Dead Knock

PETER TURNBULL

Dead Knock

ST. MARTIN'S PRESS
NEW YORK

Library of Congress Cataloging in Publication Data

Turnbull, Peter.
    Dead knock.

    I. Title.
PR6070.U68D37   1983   823'.914   82-10700
ISBN 0-312-18499-9

First published in Great Britain by William Collins Sons & Co. Ltd.

First U.S. Edition
10 9 8 7 6 5 4 3 2 1

Dead Knock

CHAPTER 1

12.30 a.m. It was Saturday—no, now it was Sunday. It had been quiet enough, for this city anyway, both Rangers and Celtic playing away had helped and so had the big march in Edinburgh. But the cells had still filled with a steady stream of quiet and occasionally good-humoured arrests. There was the one exception of the thug, now manacled to his cell wall and still kicking and cursing, who had been brought in for assault and been booked for attempted murder following his sudden production of a kitchen knife. It was the ordinary five-inch thin-bladed kitchen knife which happens to be Scotland's number one murder weapon. It might be murder if the constable didn't pull through. Sand had been poured on the blood which lay on the floor and the first cadet to appear would have to clean up the mess. The desk sergeant licked the tip of his pencil and began the *Sunday Post* crossword. His name was McKenzie, he'd got twenty-five years' service and he could tell you a thing or two about nutters, like the ned who'd just pushed a knife into the chest of Constable Green. Nutters, he reckoned, came in all shapes, and all sizes, and most appeared to be normal—at first.

He filled in three across and then tapped the end of his pencil against the desk-top. He was intrigued by the clue for one down: 'Hierarchy on the run?'. Then something made him look up. In front of the desk stood a woman. McKenzie didn't know how long she had been there, which was why they'd taken him off the streets: he'd lost his keenness.

The woman and McKenzie faced each other in silence for a few seconds. McKenzie thought there was something odd about the woman, perhaps even unreal, but couldn't see what. Suddenly he saw the obvious. The woman was out of context. There was no reason why any woman should not walk up to any sergeant in any police station on a Saturday night, but the plain truth was that it was a particular type of female, in a particular state of incapability, who got her name written on the duty incident pad, especially on a Saturday night. Usually such women were not six feet tall and did not look as though they had stopped by prior to a modelling assignment with *Harper's*, and without clothes would probably look as though they had stepped out of *Penthouse*. Usually they didn't stand quietly, moistening their lips, deferentially waiting for the desk sergeant to crack one down.

'I'd like to make a statement,' the woman said. She had a soft voice, middle-, perhaps even upper-middle-class Scots, thought McKenzie, but not high enough up the scale to be mistaken for a posh Englishwoman. No, she was a Scot all right. She had two modest diamond rings on her right hand and a gold bracelet hung on her right wrist. Her hat and coat were second-hand, the previous owner having been a leopard, or maybe even a couple of leopards.

'Yes, miss.' McKenzie pushed the newspaper aside and reached for the incident pad. He tore off three colour-coded self-carbonating sheets, set them squarely in front of him and reached for the ballpoint. It suddenly occurred to him that the woman was standing in a lot of blood-soaked sand and wasn't flinching. 'Can I have your name please, miss?' He flicked the top of the ballpoint. Some woman.

'Dominique Pahl,' said the woman with clear enunciation. Then she spelled it for the sergeant, saying each letter without pausing for thought, as does a person who is used to having to spell his or her name.

'Your address?'

'Can I make a statement?'

'Can we fill in the form?'

'I'd like to see a detective.' McKenzie took in just the faintest trace of whisky under the perfume.

'I have to fill in the form, miss. It won't take a minute.'

'I want to make a statement.'

'I know; I have to—'

'It's about a murder.'

'Who's been murdered?'

'If you were to ask that question twenty-four hours from now, the answer would be that I had been murdered.'

'Someone's going to murder you, you think?'

'I *know*, Sergeant.'

'Who?' He reached for the telephone at his side.

'I don't know why I've come here,' said the woman quietly. 'You can't help us, you couldn't offer the protection that's really needed.' She turned and walked elegantly across the foyer and into the night.

McKenzie took his hand off the phone and reached for his newspaper. They got all sorts of nutters, he thought, especially on a Saturday night, all sorts. Then he smiled and licked his pencil. One down was 'pecking order'.

Hamilton saw the woman as she turned down Renfield Street. She was tall, leopard-skin coat, matching hat, black boots. She carried herself well, upright, nice pace, not too slow, not too fast. A lady walking home, and why not? It was a good night for walking, a clear, late autumn night, a slight chill in the air and an edge on the wind, but not cold by any means. He matched her pace and followed her, one hundred yards behind and on the opposite side of the street. The woman gave a drunk a wide berth. Hamilton found nothing about the woman to arouse his curiosity, nothing to arouse his concern. He was just walking her through his patch like a good beat copper should. The woman crossed the Clyde on the Jamaica Bridge and Hamilton walked on alongside the river before turning left towards the Barrows.

The Barrowland was quiet, the city was quiet and, save for the occasional windblown paper, still. Hamilton breathed deeply. He loved this city, Big G, and he had a job which paid him to walk her streets while she was sleeping. He thought himself a lucky man. He walked the length of a long, dimly lit street so that he might enjoy a cigarette, and then walked back towards P Division station. He wanted to see if the car was still there.

It was. For some reason it intrigued him. Long after all the other cars had been driven away this one remained, neatly parked under the trees on Newton Place. He had first noticed it a few minutes before midnight and it was still there at 2 a.m. Hamilton reckoned it likely belonged to a company director who stayed out at Bearsden, who'd had too much bevvy and done the sensible thing and hailed a cab to take him home. The car sat there, gleaming in the street lights, a sleek two-door BMW in German racing silver. The leaves were beginning to pile against the tyres.

Hamilton walked back up Sauchiehall Street. Oh, this city, this city.

Monday morning was grey and overcast. The wind blew down off the Campsies and was keener than in the previous few days. It blew more leaves higher into the air and tugged more relentlessly at the trees. It was still warm enough and dry enough to do without a top coat, but winter was in the air.

At 5.45 a.m. Hamilton signed on duty. He felt knackered, already before he started he was knackered. Three different shifts, early, back, and late; he was happy with any doing a week on each, but then came the change-over and that was when it got him, always the same. Knackered. He'd signed off at 6.10 a.m. Sunday, gone home and slept like a log until 2.30 p.m., tossed around, read the *Post*, had a cup of tea, and had got up at 3 p.m. He talked with his wife and helped feed and change their son. At 5 p.m. he felt fresh, vigorous, alive, strong, fit for another shift. But the other shift didn't start until 6 a.m. Monday. He went back to bed at midnight to try and get some kip, but couldn't and only succeeded in keeping his wife awake. He had finally sunk into a fitful sleep at 3 a.m. only to be woken by a piercing alarm at 5.15. He reached P Division station at 5.45, about to start an eight-hour shift just when he felt he ought to be climbing into bed.

At 6 a.m. he formed up with the others, showed appointments, and took out his notebook as Sergeant McKenzie, with rings around his eyes, read the notices. Twelve stolen motor vehicles over the weekend, these are the numbers . . . Break-in at a jeweller's on Gibson Street, keep a look-out for a man aged about twenty-three, dark, with a scar running down his left cheek. This is the first of the month, so watch for expired tax discs on motors; pull up any motors with defective lights, the Inspector's cracking down; lighting-up time finishes at 8.30.

At 6.20 a.m. Hamilton left the station and out of curiosity walked down Sauchiehall Street towards Newton Place, just a two-minute stroll from the police station. The car was still there, the silver BMW, much the same as when Hamilton had last seen it thirty-six hours previously, except that the pile of leaves had reached the bottom of the hub caps. Hamilton approached the car. It had a new registration and the sticker of a large West Scotland motor dealer in the back window. Both doors were locked. There appeared to be nothing inside the car save for a copy of the *Lady* on the rear seat. The car was nose-in on a single yellow line and at 8 a.m. would be in violation of the parking restrictions, but Hamilton saw no reason to wait. No company director has a hangover which lasts that long, and no one leaves a few thousand pounds'-worth of precision engineering unattended in the centre of any city for that amount of time. He gripped the radio attached to his uniform collar and radioed in details of the vehicle. He returned to his beat, looking for motors with expired tax discs and defective lighting, and trying to wake as the bitch city awoke around him.

The terminal of the Police National Computer identified the car as being registered to one Dominique Pahl of 188 Matilda Avenue, Pollokshields. Always a thorough man and sharing his generation's distrust of computers, Sergeant McKenzie double-checked the name and address on the electoral register and also with the city's street index. Only then did he detail a unit to call at 188 Matilda Avenue as a matter of routine enquiry.

Tango Delta Foxtrot was a low-slung Ford, white with an orange flash, two blue lights on the roof and new Yankee-style 'woofer' sirens under the bonnet. Sophisticated electronic gadgetry and the car's general state of maintenance made its value double that of similar models in the showrooms. It was not difficult to estimate the cash value of Tango Delta Foxtrot, but the value of having the unit on the streets at all was inestimable. PCs Wooler and Brocker worked Tango Delta Foxtrot and between them they had amassed twelve years of police experience. All in all, Tango Delta Foxtrot was a big, big asset.

The early part of the shift PCs Wooler and Brocker spent supervising the traffic on the westbound carriageway of the M8, which in the morning rush-hour had all the fluency of a blocked drain. That morning there were three shunts and the additional complication of a broken-down juggernaut. The traffic began to flow again at 9.30 a.m. At 9.35 Tango Delta Foxtrot investigated a fight at a hostel for down-and-outs, at 10.05 it responded to a three-nines call for a fire appliance, at 10.42 it stopped and booked a woman for dangerous driving. Wooler and Brocker didn't start on their list of routine calls until 11 a.m. They didn't get around to calling at 188 Matilda Avenue until 11.30.

188 Matilda Avenue was a detached house just a little too small to be called a mansion. It was the kind of property that is invoked in Glasgow v. Edinburgh debates by way of example to show that for all its violence, squalor, deprivation and unemployment, Glasgow also happens to be ten times wealthier than the toy town on the Forth. 188 Matilda Avenue had two tall stone gateposts and a long drive which opened out into a car-park in front of the main door. The front garden was landscaped in a series of terraces down towards the roadway. The building seemed to have been repainted and repointed and looked good for another three or four winters.

Wooler drove up the driveway, turned in a wide circle and halted in front of the main door. As they turned they glanced into the bay window; the room had chesterfields, walls lined with books, a leopard-skin coat on the table, and there was a woman sitting in a chair.

Inside a dog was barking frantically, but no one answered the door. Brocker walked to the bay window and tapped on the glass. The woman was sitting upright, but she didn't turn when Brocker drummed his finger-nails on the pane. Then the dog, a labrador, ran into the room in front of the woman and started barking at Brocker. Still the woman didn't move. The door was eight feet tall and six feet wide, and was made of oak studded with metal. Wooler and Brocker went in through the window.

Lee Sung took delivery of the three crates of prawns just as he had taken delivery of three crates of prawns every

Monday morning for the last twelve months. The van was the same as always, the old and battered blue Transit, and the driver was the same, the well-built young man who was always willing to help with the unloading. It was just the weather that was on the change. Lee Sung always knew when winter was coming; his right leg told him with a dull but constant pain which would only go away when the spring came. He couldn't even reminisce about the warm winters in the old country; Lee Sung had been born and brought up in Dundee.

He and the driver carried the prawns to the rear of the shop, Lee Sung leading the way, limping with one box, and the driver following carrying two boxes. Lee Sung signed the delivery invoice and the driver left the shop. The three crates lay on the bench, a few hundred ice-packed frozen prawns which had to be transferred to the deep freeze. Wearily Lee Sung grasped the wrench and set to work. Already his fingers were numb and the pain in his leg was beginning to sharpen. The crates were the same, light-coloured wood, bounded by steel rings, and marked, as they had always been, 'Kedderman, Rotterdam'. On each crate was the Customs clearance stamp. The contents were the same, rock-hard pink prawns and ice crystals. It was the additions that puzzled Lee Sung. In each crate were two packets; small, cylindrical in shape, two inches long and about one inch across, made of heavy-duty black plastic and sealed at both ends. He laid the packets aside as he came to them; he just wanted to get the lousy prawns into the lousy freezer fast.

Half an hour later he'd finished the job and went to the back of the shop to chuck out the bits of crate and mop up the water made by the melting ice. He leaned the mop against the wall and turned his attention to the six black packets. They were small, but solidly packed and heavy for their size. They were unmarked. He tried to undo the seal but could not, so he took a knife and punctured one of the packets. A fine white powder spilled on to the shelf. Lee Sung hadn't always been in the catering trade, and the sight of the white powder wrapped him in a chill worse than any Scottish winter. Horse; White Elephant; it was the same in any language, it meant a lot of money and a lot of ruined humanity. Lee Sung made a three-nines call.

Poppa Fox India was there in two minutes: DC Dick King arrived three minutes later. One of the constables from the unit picked up the black packages and dropped them gingerly into a large envelope. Then he scraped the white powder that had spilled when Lee Sung punctured the packet into a self-sealing sachet. The other constable gathered up the wood that had contained the prawns, carried it back through the shop and put it in the boot of Poppa Fox India. Dick King talked with Lee Sung.

'Who made the delivery, Mr Sung?'

'Same as always. Scot Euro Imports. Same as always.'

'Down in the docks, right?' King scribbled in his notebook.

'I don't know. Down in the telephone cable is all I know.'

'You got the number?'

'Four-four-oh, one-three-two-one.' Lee Sung reeled off the number from memory.

'Four-four-oh is the code for Govan,' said King. 'That's the docks.'

'Wouldn't know,' replied Lee Sung, moving over towards the electric heater and rubbing his leg. 'I've never had reason to go to them. They're the only seafood import company in this city that operates a local delivery service. That's why he uses them.'

'He?'

'My brother. He owns this joint.'

'Getting them delivered is cheaper than fetching them, is it?'

'We don't run a vehicle and they only charge ten pence on the pound for delivery.'

'Uh-huh. How long have you been using them?'

'Around two years.'

'Always reliable?'

'I've only been here for the last twelve months. In that time they've been OK.'

'OK?'

'They deliver on time. The latest driver helps with the unloading. They're OK.'

'So tell me about the driver.'

'He's OK.'

'You said that. Tell me what OK means.'

'He helps out. Not like the last guy. A real crabbit cretin was the last guy.'

'All right, so this is the first time anything like this has happened?'

'Oh, it happens twice a day, only I thought I'd relieve the boredom and tell you this time.'

'Don't get wise. It's never happened before?'

'No.'

'Your brother around, is he?'

'He's sleeping upstairs. He and his wife work this place in the evenings, I heave the stock around and throw out the crap in the mornings.'

'I'd like to talk to him.'

'He doesn't speak good English. He's only interested in what comes out of the TV on the counter and what goes into the till. His wife doesn't even speak any.'

'Where'd you get your English?'

'Wandsworth. I did seven of ten. Big M. I was fitted up.'

'Course you were,' said King.

King checked the address of Scot Euro Imports in Lee Sung's telephone directory, and drove to Govan. There were days, he remembered, not so long ago, less than fifteen years, when the big freighters were stacked in lines in the estuary, waiting for weeks for an unloading berth; a time when money was in good supply and nobody seemed to observe Sundays. King drove down the greasy, pitted, cobbled road between the warehouses. His was the only vehicle on the road; the warehouses were empty, the cranes were still. There was just one ship, an old freighter with rusting plates, tied up in the Regent's Basin, which served to show that the river still had some life.

Scot Euro Imports owned a warehouse at the far end of the docks at the point where the quays gave way to the rusting slipways of liquidated shipbuilding yards. The large doors of the warehouse were painted green; a smaller door, set in one of the large doors, was painted yellow. King pushed open the yellow door. Inside the warehouse were banks of industrial deep-freezing equipment, a garden-type shed, and a fifteen-hundred-weight van. The floor was uneven and puddles had formed in the depressions. In front of the van two men were playing cards. They sat on three-legged stools and slapped the cards down hard on to the side of an empty tea-chest. One of the men was middle-aged and spreading vastly about his midriff, the other was young, blond, and seemed to King to be in good shape. They looked up as King approached them.

'Police,' said King and held up his ID card.

'That's all we need,' said the older of the two.

'Twist,' said the younger man.

The old man laid his hand face-down on the tea-chest.

'You make deliveries of prawns?' asked King. He heard his voice echo in the vastness of the warehouse.

'He asks if we make deliveries of prawns.' The older man spread his arms, palms upwards. 'Sure we make deliveries of prawns. You want to buy my business maybe?'

'Police,' said King. 'I told you.'

'So you still maybe want to to buy me out?'

'They don't buy anything, Mr David,' said the younger man.

'For years I've been waiting for someone to buy my business. You're not just a little interested?'

King shook his head. 'I want to see your list of deliveries.'

'He wants to see my list of deliveries. Listen, I'm a businessman, you say that to somebody and he'll think, wealth, riches, ay, ay, ay,' said the older man with an air of resignation. 'I've got a daughter who is looking like the back end from a bus and I have to find someone to marry her. What with, eh, what with?' He turned his palms upwards again. 'I had money, it went on my son's barmitzvah. When he's out of school already I throw all this up, believe me, and I'll work as a parking warden. It pays lousy, but it's regular; this pays lousy, but it's not regular. I've been wanting to sell for years, so when providence sends a stranger to my door all he wants is for to see my list of deliveries. Ay, ay, ay, you're not just a little interested?'

'Just the deliveries.'

'I'll throw in a van that's beat-up more than any van's got the right to be beat-up.'

'Deliveries!'

'Deliveries. Deliveries is in the office. Some office, eh? A garden shed with a view of the warehouse, tons and tons of frozen pink things, and sometimes some octopus or squid to liven things up.'

The man stood with some effort and ambled round the back of the van towards the wooden hut.

'You do the deliveries?' asked King.

'That's right,' replied the younger man. 'Just me and me.'

'Notice anything strange about the deliveries this morning?'

'No, why?' He smiled. For some reason King didn't like the smile.

'Where do you deliver to? The areas, I mean.'

'I work at my own route. I start with the ones far out; Cumbernauld, Falkirk, Chinky joints mostly. Some Pakis. Mostly Chink. I drive out, then drive back into Glasgow, unloading on the way.'

'How do you know which boxes go to which restaurants?'

'Or take-aways. Most of our customers are take-away joints.'

'OK.'

'We don't know. I mean, all the boxes are the same. We deal in prawns mostly, sometimes other fish, but mostly prawns. So the customer just orders so many crates of prawns, say he wants two, then I unload the two nearest the door of the van. Simple.'

'Couldn't be simpler.'

'They've got some writing on, the crates, but those wogs they can't read. They can't lift either, I do it for them. Some of them they slay me, whole families, tribes, Chinks and Pakis, swarming around the van, couldn't organize a bevvy in a brewery.'

'That's your opinion,' said King coldly, 'only don't use those words.'

'What words? Bevvy?'

'Pakis and Chinks,' said King. 'I don't like it.'

'Listen, will you, I'm telling you, if I was prejudiced you could say that, but I'm not prejudiced. Why do I help them if I'm prejudiced? Tell me that. I got nothing against them, Jim, nothing. They want to come over here and make a bit and bring all their wives, who's to stop them. Not me. They keep themselves to themselves, Chinks and Pakis, I like that, so long as they behave I don't mind, I'll even help them unload. Niggers, we don't have many niggers in Big G, but they're coming.

When the niggers — '

King kicked the stool from under him. The boy fell into a puddle, rolled over and glared at King, who said, 'I don't like that word either.'

'That boy is a clumsy one,' said the older man from behind the van. 'He is getting clumsier each day, believe me.'

'Did you see that, Mr David?' The boy's voice was high-pitched.

'See what, Donny?' replied the older man, walking around the front of the van. 'I haven't seen anything in years. Not even money.' He handed a sheet of paper to King. It listed fifteen restaurants and take-aways in the Greater Glasgow area. 'That's the morning run. Donny does an afternoon run. That goes west; Greenock for three drops. Then to Kilmarnock and Ayr. You want that list?'

'Not at the moment. How many more crates have you got from this particular batch?'

'Donny, how many?'

'Dunno,' said the boy shortly, still looking at King. 'Twenty-six, twenty-seven.'

'When did you take delivery?'

'They cleared Customs on Thursday morning and we took delivery on Thursday afternoon, well, maybe more like lunch-time Thursday.'

'Where do the prawns come from?'

'Holland.'

'Where in Holland?'

'Rotterdam. So why?' asked the older man.

'We had a complaint about the quality of the product,' said King. 'Foreign bodies getting in and spoiling the taste.'

'And *that* means police action?'

'Contravention of the Public Health Act,' said King. 'So tell me again, you make all your deliveries and all the

crates are the same.'
'Yes,' said the younger man.
'No,' said the older man.
They both looked at each other.
'The woman,' said the older man.
'I was forgetting her,' replied the younger man.
'The way you look at her, how can you forget her?'
'Tell me about her,' said King.
'We don't deliver to all our customers and all the crates are not the same,' said the older man. 'The woman is a classy piece, fur coat, expensive car. She collects a dozen crates once a month, last Friday in each month. She owns a restaurant. She has to.'
'Name?'
'Miss Pahl, lives in Matilda Avenue in the south side. I don't have the number right off-hand.'
'She calls every month?'
'Yes. For the last eighteen months. Once a month, last Friday, pays in cash.'
King scribbled in his notebook. 'And her crates were different?'
'Only in that they had a red sticker on them. No real difference — one spilled once, and we saw the contents — well, Donny did, 'cos he helped to repack it — just the same prawns, solidly frozen. But she was so worried about the breakage.' The older man nodded reflectively. 'She couldn't have been more worried if she was looking into the barrel of a gun, believe me.'
'She always picked the ones with the red sticker?'
'We had to leave them aside for her.'
'They just had stickers? What were they like?'
' 'Bout as big as a tenpenny piece, with writing on.'
'Writing? What sort of writing?'
The older man shrugged. 'Chinese writing.'
'And they cleared Customs?' King was amazed.
'The whole batch gets cleared, prawns from

Rotterdam, once a week, comes round like pay-day.'

'Only once a month there's twelve crates with little red stickers on them. You didn't think to report it?'

The older man made an appealing gesture. 'I have to make a living,' he said.

'OK. So Miss Pahl in the fast car comes once a month, so she came last Friday, three days ago.'

'Right,' said the older man. 'She took six crates, then came back for six more. She must know when they come in, her crates are only in the freezer for a few hours before she collects.'

'You couldn't mix her crates up by mistake?'

'No time,' said the older man, 'she's often here before we have time to get them put aside for her. She helps look them out.'

'Anyway,' said the young man icily, 'our unloading procedure wouldn't allow it.'

'Our unloading procedure, will you listen?' The older man raised his head towards the roof. 'Our unloading procedure, he makes me sound more like a multinational each day, believe me. You have too many big ideas, Donny, you are a Glasgow boy who is coming from Partick, some day you should remember that, Donny. Last week one customer is screaming on the phone for his order and so Donny, Donny my boy, he tells him the van is — what did you say, Donny? — in the ongoing vehicle maintenance section for emergency repairs, would you believe? The ongoing vehicle maintenance section is Donny in overalls fiddling with the carburettor, ay, ay, ay.' The man raised his hands again, palms upwards. 'But that is not enough, then he must go and tell the customer that it may be possible to despatch the order in another vehicle from the fleet. That van, there, beat up more than any van has the right to be beat up, that is my fleet in its entirety. I use it on Sundays to take my family out. Can you see anything being delivered in an emergency in that? Donny, I'm a poor man, give me peace.'

'You need to raise your sights, Mr David,' said the younger man.

'They are raised. I'm going to be a traffic warden with a yellow cap.'

'Try looking at your own windscreen,' said King. 'As from midnight yesterday your tax disc has expired. Tell me about the loading procedure.'

'Ay, ay, ay, so now it's the tax, more expense. The loading procedure, what Donny means is we load the crates one by one on the floor of the van, then load others on top, layer by layer.'

'One at a time,' said the younger man. 'We couldn't help but notice any red stickers. I also unload from the back to the front, so we'd see any stickers on the side as well as any on the top.'

'I see,' said King. 'Can I take your names, gentlemen?'

'David Bauermeister.'

'Donald McFarlane.'

Bauermeister gave an address in Eastwood; King thought he probably wasn't so destitute. McFarlane gave an address in Partick.

'One other thing,' said King, folding his notebook. 'No more deliveries today, please. Keep your stock here. We might want to check it out.'

'My customers . . .' sighed Bauermeister. King stared at him and Bauermeister sighed again.

In his car, King radioed in the addresses of the fifteen restaurants to which Donald McFarlane had made deliveries that morning. Ray Sussock took the call and crossed Lee Sung's restaurant off the list. Fourteen remained, and any or all might have taken a delivery of something more than prawns that morning which would have to be investigated immediately. Cars were despatched to ten of the fourteen, which lay within Strathclyde; details of the remaining four were passed to the Central Region police. Over the next three-quarters of an hour the cars reported in: five restaurants had found packages in the prawns. One restaurateur had flushed them down his toilet, thinking they were cooling agents for the period of transit and now redundant; another had thrown them away with the refuse, where they were recovered; and three restaurateurs had simply laid them aside, not recognizing them as anything useful to the efficient running of a commercial enterprise. All recovered packages were on their way to P Division by special courier.

Sussock typed up the results of the calls to the restaurants and took his report to Donoghue's office.

Donoghue, impeccably dressed, was leaning back in his chair and pulling on his pipe. The smoke in the room made Sussock's chest hurt. Donoghue motioned for Sussock to sit in the chair in front of his desk.

'Something big?' asked Sussock.

'I think so, Ray,' replied Donoghue, without taking the pipe from his mouth. He held Sussock's report in the air while he read it. 'So five restaurants had packages in the prawns. Six, counting the one in Sauchiehall Street.'

'Has the analysis been confirmed yet, sir?'

'Oh yes, it's heroin all right. Bothwell phoned in from the forensic lab. a few minutes ago. It's very, very good stuff apparently.'

'Value?'

'Probably about half a million pounds on the street, according to the Met. Drugs Squad. I phoned down about an hour ago and tried to describe what we had. The bloke on the other end reckoned the value to be about five to ten thousand pounds per packet, depending on the degree of cut.'

'Cut?'

'Amount of impurity. So if we have thirty-six packets of good quality heroin, say ten thousand per packet . . .'

'Three hundred and sixty thousand pounds'-worth,' said Sussock. 'Somebody's head's going to roll.'

'I think it already has, Ray.'

'Oh?'

Donoghue slid a sheet of paper across the desk towards Sussock. Sussock picked it up.

JR/CT   Dept of Pathology
                                        Glasgow Royal Infirmary

                                     1st November

P Division
Strathclyde Police
Glasgow
G3

REPORT ON POST-MORTEM OF PERSON BELIEVED TO BE DOMINIQUE PAHL

On the morning of the first of November I attended the dwelling-house at 188 Matilda Avenue, Pollokshields at the request of Chief Superintendent Findlater. I found the above-named deceased to be sitting in a chair. The skin of the deceased was punctured on the left forearm. I could see no apparent cause of death and so asked permission to remove the body to the laboratory for post-mortem. Permission was given by Inspector Donoghue, senior officer at the scene.

Results of Post-Mortem

(1)   The body is that of a female Caucasian. Apparent age: thirty years. Rigor Mortis established.

(2)   Time of death (allowing for room temperature of 8° Celsius which would have arrested progress of

rigor mortis) approx. 36 hours before post-mortem.

(3) A reddening of lower lumbar region and buttocks caused by settling of red blood corpuscles after death. This would indicate deceased had died in the sitting position in which she was found.

(4) Traces of large dose of pure heroin estimated at 200mg. This would probably cause a profound comatose condition and lower the respiratory rate. Pupils dilated. Skeletal muscles flaccid, tongue had fallen back and blocked the airway. Death was due to respiratory failure.

(5) Deceased had given birth by Caesarian section 3-5 years previously.

Dr P Reynolds
Dept of Pathology

'You think they're connected, sir?' Sussock put the PM report back on to Donoghue's desk.

'Can't fail to be, Ray.' He stood and reached for his top-coat. 'Is King back from the warehouse yet?'

'He's typing up his report.'

'Montgomerie?' Donoghue buttoned his coat.

'He'll be in in half an hour. He's out at the break-in at the jeweller's.'

'Where do the prawns come from, Ray?'

'An export company in Rotterdam. King has the name.'

'Telex the Netherlands Police for information, please, Ray. Give them everything we've got. Don't let King sign off, we've got a meeting with Chief Superintendent Findlater at 5 p.m. Tell Montgomerie to be there as well. Just to kick around what we've got.'

'Will do,' said Sussock.

Donoghue walked up Sauchiehall Street to his favourite

tobacconist's at the corner of George Square. He stood and looked at the pipes in the display cabinet while his mix was being made up: a Dutch base for taste, with a twist of dark shag for depth of flavour and a slower burning rate. He was kicking around what he had. He had half a million pounds'-worth of high-grade heroin suddenly appear in a city with no big narcotics problem. He had a woman in the prime of life who had driven her sports coupé into the city, had a couple of drinks and then gone to the police station with the intention of asking for protection 'for us' but had only got as far as giving the desk sergeant her name. She had then walked out of the police station and strolled back to her palatial mansion. There she had waited for someone to kill her and had seemingly put up no resistance while her sleeve was rolled up and a syringe full of heroin solution was injected into her vein.

Monday. Monday.

CHAPTER 2

Monday: 5.10 p.m.

Donoghue, Sussock, Montgomerie and King sat on chairs which had been arranged in a semi-circle in front of Chief Superintendent Findlater's desk. To the side of the group and sitting in a chair which had been pushed against the wall was WPC Willems. A notebook rested on her lap in which she scribbled shorthand notes. Findlater was a bald Highlander with a gigantic frame, whose huge hands made sheets of A4 look like postage stamps. He read the reports and listened to the verbal contributions. Then he said, 'It's gangland.' Donghue looked at the ceiling.

'What do you suggest, Inspector?' Findlater appealed

to Donoghue. He spoke in a smooth Highland accent that held no trace of alarm or hurry. Findlater in fact rarely hurried, and the pace at which he had built his career seemed to be one of a slow, deliberate plod, which had taken him from the quiet streets of Elgin to the position of Chief Superintendent in Glasgow in an honourable thirty years. He also had a gentleness about him which cynics reckoned was because he had never known a fight. All confrontations Findlater had been involved in, it was said, were over before he had time to clench his fists, because only a lunatic would go up against a man who stood like an oak tree and moved like an iceberg.

'I want to search the house at Matilda Avenue, turn it inside out. King's report confirms that the woman, Dominique Pahl, picked up heroin every month. Somehow this month's consignment went astray and it's my guess that she was killed, murdered, because of it. The organization meting out its own justice.'

'So there's a murderer in the city?' Findlater leafed through the reports.

'I think so,' replied Donoghue. He glanced out of the window. 5.15, the lights on Sauchiehall Street were being switched on. 'Killing this woman must have left a vacancy, there should be some activity.'

'Not necessarily any that would point a finger at our wee pal with the syringe.' Findlater laid the reports on his desk and rested his fleshy hands on them. 'He's probably long gone by now.'

'Probably, but we can't assume that.'

'They've probably all gone by now,' said King. 'This has blown their cover, they'll have packed their bags and hoofed it.'

'Again, probably,' said Donoghue, reaching into his jacket pocket for his pipe. 'We can't close a case because of a probability; anyway, I'm not sure they have flown, they wouldn't have done such a neat and clueless job on

Ms Pahl unless they intended to stick around. I think they'll change the cosmetics of the organization, but its nature will remain.'

'So we have heroin importers and a dab hand with a syringe,' grunted Findlater. 'What a way to start the week.'

Donoghue turned to King. 'What feelings did you get about the two guys in Scot Euro Imports, Bauermeister and the van-boy?'

'The old man seemed on the up-and-up,' replied King. 'I'm not sure about the other one.'

'That comes out in your report. Didn't like him, did you?'

'Frankly, no.'

'He didn't read quite right, even allowing for your prejudice. I think we ought to watch him for a while, sir.'

'A surveillance?' asked Findlater.

'Uh-huh.' Donoghue grunted and attempted to light his pipe, but without success.

'That's expensive. It's a bad use of man-hours and I'm under pressure to cut costs.'

'I know, sir —'

'Our budget takes us from April to April, we've got another five months to go and we've overspent already.' He reached into his in-tray and pulled out a sheet of paper. 'Look, this has come down from Region. I'm having it circulated. It's a memo telling us that from now on we've got to use two sides of bits of paper. It's got down to that level.'

'For heaven's sake,' hissed Sussock under his breath, and Montgomerie grinned at him.

'You reckon you can justify a surveillance in this economic climate?' growled Findlater.

'Yes, sir,' said Donoghue quietly and calmly. 'I think it's necessary.'

'Very well.' Findlater relented and allowed himself a

smile. 'When do you expect the Telex reply from the Dutch police?'

'Should come in during the next two hours, sir,' replied Sussock.

'What have we got for action, Constable?' Findlater turned to WPC Willems.

'Surveillance on van-boy and—' she paused while she flicked over the pages of her notebook—'further investigation of the house at Matilda Avenue.'

'Should keep you busy,' said Findlater, folding the file in front of him. 'Inspector Donoghue to co-ordinate the enquiry. Do try to keep me informed this time, Inspector. You can start by letting me see the reply from the Netherlands police when it comes in.'

'I will, sir,' said Donoghue, putting his lighter to his pipe for a second time, and with more success.

5.38: Close of conference. 5.42: Car pool. 6.04: On station outside Scot Euro Imports. Montgomerie filled in his notebook, settled down in the driver's seat and looked out under the steering-wheel at the old warehouse, the greasy cobbles and the dim sodium lamps against the night sky. The only time he had recorded with accuracy was the last one, the others were approximations and he had chosen odd times to add a stamp of authenticity. Early in his days as a policeman Montgomerie had realized that being good at your job was important, but appearing to be good at it was essential. He had no idea when the conference in Chief Superintendent Findlater's office had closed, but he reasoned Donoghue did not know either.

6.10: Subject and Bauermeister leave warehouse together in 15-cwt van, Bauermeister driving.

The van rattled past Montgomerie, who buried his head in a road atlas. He let the van go round the corner at the far end of the road before turning his car in a tight U and accelerating after it. Bauermeister drove the old van slowly eastwards along Govan Road, and Montgomerie, in a black car and using only side lights, hung close. Bauermeister turned left on to Paisley Road and then hung a suicidal right against the rush-hour traffic to cross the river by the Kingston Bridge. Montgomerie stuck like glue. The van turned left at Charing Cross, driving under the shadow of P Division station, and down into Partick. Montgomerie glanced at the station as he drove by; he saw Donoghue leaning against the windowsill, pulling on his pipe and reading a case file.

6.39: Van stops at junction of Dumbarton Road and Church Street. Subject alights.

Montgomerie left the car on a double trouble and followed McFarlane as he strolled slowly through the crowd in a gloom pierced by shop-window lights, street lamps and cars' headlights. McFarlane looked like any young guy returning home after a day's work. He walked across Byres Road and into Lawrence Street. Lawrence Street was empty; long and empty. It was a street made up of solid sandstone terraces, one side of which had been recently sandblasted, and the stone on that side of the street glowed in its original light-orange hue. The other side of the street had not been cleaned and the stonework was the usual late-twentieth-century black. Montgomerie dropped back and walked on the dark side of the street. McFarlane reached the end of the street, skirted a group of children who were playing skip with an old hosepipe, and turned into Hyndland Crescent. Montgomerie crossed over the road, jogged to the corner, and turned into Hyndland Crescent in time to see McFarlane walk into the close mouth of 197. Montgomerie crossed on to the opposite side of the street. There were six flats on the stair; four already had lights on. Montgomerie waited. The lights of the top flat were suddenly switched on and McFarlane appeared at the window and tugged the curtains shut.

6.46: Subject enters house at 197 Hyndland Crescent, top right.

Montgomerie walked quickly back to Dumbarton Road and drove his car off the yellow lines. He hadn't collected a ticket. He took the car to Hyndland Crescent and stopped on the opposite side of the road to 197, six closes down. For the second time that evening he settled down in the driver's seat and studied the world from under the steering-wheel. Cars were being parked at the kerb, people were walking up the road and turning into closes, lights were being switched on. Hyndland Crescent was coming home. Montgomerie shifted in his seat. He was growing uncomfortable and his backside was getting numb. It was getting numb because it was small and had no excess flesh. It was one of the things about him that girls fancied, that and his blue eyes deep set below bushy eyebrows, his dark complexion and downturned moustache, small hips, flat stomach and strong shoulders. Since he was seventeen he had had his pick of women and at twenty-six it was getting even easier. But they tended to cling, become possessive and made him feel claustrophobic.

He shifted his position on the car seat and began to look out over the top of the steering-wheel. The lights were still on in McFarlane's flat but there had been no other sign of him. Montgomerie lit a fag and wondered how he could tell Fiona it was off. He'd done it before, so why was it so difficult with Fiona? The direct approach was best, it was the quickest way to achieve that delicious flush of relief which comes with regained freedom. Listen, Fiona, it's off, all over. OK?

Not OK.

It was the little things that got him about Fiona. The way she moved, the curious lilt in her voice. Or was it? He suspected he remembered the little things because he couldn't bring himself to admit his need for the other things Fiona offered; her beauty, intellect, warmth, love. Love. She also had the priceless virtue of enabling Montgomerie to find his freedon in their relationship. He thought he remembered the little things because he didn't want to admit to the awful truth. He would go and see her the next evening, probably even broach the subject, but he knew that she would sink into his arms and his hand would slide up her back to the zip of her dress and he would end up staying the night. Again.

7.37: Subject leaves flat and takes car, reg. no. DMF 1000.

Some car. A low-slung black Granada with tinted windows. McFarlane drove along Dumbarton Road, on to Argyle Street and into the city. He drove slowly and carefully, gliding the huge Dagenham sledge sedately through the traffic. Montgomerie trailed three vehicles behind, not too concerned about losing sight of McFarlane because there couldn't be too many heaps like that on the town that night. McFarlane turned into Ingram Street and drove down Albion Street, hung a right on to Candleriggs and back on to Ingram.

7.51: Subject halts outside the Antonine Hotel. Alights from vehicle and enters hotel.

Montgomerie ran his car on to the pavement and halted a hundred yards behind McFarlane's vehicle. It occurred to him that McFarlane's heap was carrying a personalized registration number.

7.57: Subject leaves hotel with female companion.

McFarlane was dressed in a velvet jacket and smart trousers. In fact, he looked pretty Gucci'd up. The woman on his arm was no chicken; mid thirties, slim, shortish, long fur coat over an evening gown, gold and diamonds round her neck and rocks on most fingers. McFarlane opened the front passenger door of the Granada and the woman slid on to the seat with practised grace and elegance.

The show they went to see was at the top right flat, 197 Hyndland Crescent. Or possibly it was an exclusive restaurant. Whatever it was, they enjoyed each other's company until a taxi arrived at eleven-thirty to take the lady away.

Midnight: light in flat switched off.

00.30: No indication of subject being active. Leaving observation.

Montgomerie stopped off at an all-night grill and bought a meat pie. He reckoned Donald McFarlane had some social life for a van-boy.

The big house was guarded by a single constable who saluted smartly as Donoghue and King approached. He stepped aside and Donoghue pushed open the main door. It was heavy, but swung smoothly on its hinges. Inside, dim bulbs reluctantly gave light and the polished oak panelling absorbed more than it reflected. The dark carpets didn't help either. The two men moved quietly through to the front room where Dominique Pahl had been found sitting with a fully relaxed tongue blocking her airway.

It was a large room with brighter lights than the hall and with more oak panelling covering the bottom half of all four walls. The ceiling was patterned with ornate plasterwork, the carpet was new and not cheap, the furniture was two chesterfield settees with two matching chairs, a Welsh dresser and a tall bookcase.

'She was found in that chair,' said Donoghue, indicating the chair which faced away from the window. 'Sitting upright with her hands resting on her lap.'

'And there was no sign of a struggle?' King looked at Donoghue.

'None. No sign of a break-in either. She must have waited for the murderer to come to her and she let him, or her, inject her with the stuff. She just accepted her own execution. Can you imagine the power someone must have held over her to force such resignation?'

Richard King confessed he could not.

'So he filled her full of pure heroin and her whole muscle tone relaxed and her tongue sagged back and blocked her throat. But it didn't happen without violence; the doctor reckons the lacerations on her tongue were caused by a convulsion, she was probably blown off the chair. So he picks her up and puts her back in the chair, smooths out the creases, and leaves while her muscles are beginning to relax.'

'Straight past the dog.'

'The dog was only there to bark and maybe for a bit of company. It's apparently settled in with the next-door family without too much fuss, and anyway a professional killer would know how to cope with a guard dog. You approach them with confidence and talk softly.'

'That simple,' said King. 'Did she own the house?'

'According to the deeds it was hers all right. Whether she put up the money or not is another matter.'

'Did Forensic find anything?'

Donoghue shook his head. 'Jimmy Bothwell must have spread a ton of aluminium powder but he only found her fingerprints and a few blank smudges, no doubt left by the gloved hands of the killer. Other than that just dog hairs. Take a seat, King.'

King sat on the settee, sinking into the soft polished hide. Donoghue sat in one of the chairs. It seemed fitting to King that Donoghue chose a chair.

'What are we here for?' asked Donoghue, putting his pipe to his mouth.

'To search the house?' King was curious.

'What are we looking for? What would you look for?'

'I don't know. Anything which will help us establish her identity.'

'I think we know who she is.'

'I meant anything that will help us to find out how she filled in her days, what she did on the other twenty-nine or so days of each month, and where she sent the heroin. Anyway, I'm not sure we do know her identity.'

Donoghue smiled and lit his pipe. 'I'm glad you said that.'

'We know a name, that's all.'

'I'm fairly certain it will be her real name. We need to know about her background. We must find out where her child is.'

'We need an address book, that sort of thing.'

'That would help.'

'Photograph albums and the like.'

'Right. That's one area of search; I do like to do things methodically, King. I've little time for goons who rip everything to shreds and just bury information under the mess they've created. What else are we looking for?'

'Information connected with the heroin. That could be anything.'

'Or anywhere. So we don't dismiss anything as insignificant. A timetable of events might help.'

'This is Monday, Monday evening,' said King. 'She picked up the consignment on Friday morning. That is, she picked up a dozen boxes with red labels on them. She came to the station at midnight on Saturday, so sometime between Friday morning and late Saturday night she found out about the cock-up.'

'When did she find out? Not before she had all twelve crates presumably, or she would have either returned to the warehouse in a panic or not returned at all. As it is she took six in her car and returned for six more.'

'Just like normal.'

'Right. So she can't shift any more than six crates in her BMW. So she has to transfer them to a larger vehicle which takes them where?'

'And where does the transfer take place?'

'Neighbours may help. You hardly see anybody on streets in areas like this, but not a lot goes unnoticed. Anyway, the transfer takes places at some place unknown and the prawns are driven to their destination, again unknown.' He pulled on his pipe and blue smoke rose lazily towards the ceiling. 'They arrive and are broken open — no black packages despite the small red stickers, and the news is relayed to the by now doomed Miss Pahl.'

'We still don't know when,' said King. 'It could still be any time on Friday or Saturday.'

'Do you think so?' Donoghue's pipe had gone out and he examined the bowl, prodding the contents with his little finger. 'Did you read the desk officer's report?'

King nodded.

'Did it not strike you that she was coming on impulse, even allowing for the fact that she may have stopped off at a bar on the way? That she only decided it was useless to ask for protection after she had got as far as giving her name?'

'As if she had just heard about the cock-up?'

Donoghue grunted. 'Her immediate reaction was to go to the police. If she had thought about it she would have reached the decision she only reached at the desk at half past midnight yesterday. It takes half an hour to drive from here to the city; the desk sergeant said she had been drinking, she may have taken a drink here, but allowing for the fact she may have gone to a bar or a hotel I'd say she received a telephone call sometime before eleven on Saturday evening.'

'Which implies the prawns were unloaded some distance away.'

'Uh-huh.' Donoghue re-lit his pipe. 'Then she walked back and waited for somebody to kill her. She probably sat waiting in this very chair. Dr Reynolds's report indicates she died about thirty-six hours before she was found, which means that once she had returned home she

wouldn't have very long to wait. The killer may even have
been waiting for her.'

King swallowed hard. The coldness of it; just roll up
your sleeve, please, don't struggle, this won't hurt a
bit . . .

'Upset you?' asked Donoghue.

King nodded.

'Callous, isn't it?'

'Give me a nice uncomplicated stabbing in the home
any day.'

'That won't stretch you. This will. Findlater was wrong
when he said that this is gangland. It's more than
gangland, this is international crime, right here in our
fair city.'

'We're going to need assistance.'

'All we can get. But we'll do as much as we can. I
suggest you start with the house. I'll go and chat with the
neighbours.'

Donoghue left the house and walked down the
driveway. He stood on the pavement in front of the two
stone gateposts and looked about him. All the houses on
Matilda Avenue were large; some had been turned into
offices, others had been split into two or three self-
contained flatlets. All had expansive, mature gardens.

Only three other houses could offer clear views of the
comings and goings of 188 Matilda Avenue; the two on
either side and the one directly facing it on the opposite
side of the road. The house on the left was the one in
which lived the family who had taken the dog. It was a
busy house, two or three children and a well-kept garden.
Probably too busy to notice much of Ms Pahl's day-to-day
existence. The other house to the right was similarly well
kept. The curtains were open, the lights on, a man in a
dinner jacket was standing in the window holding a glass
of wine and staring out into the night. Not being able to
see anything, he turned away. There was a Rolls-Royce in

the driveway. It seemed another house which was too busy to be inquisitive.

The house opposite seemed more promising. The garden was rambling and untidy and the house looked poorly maintained. It seemed to Donoghue to be the property of an elderly person, but the lights in the upstairs rooms indicated that the owner of the house was still ambulant. He crossed over the road and walked down the driveway. Weeds grew thickly in the gravel, and shrubs stood at either side. Donoghue stepped up to the front door and pressed the bell.

A few moments passed and then through the frosted glass he saw a shadow moving in the hallway. The lock clicked and a bolt was drawn. The door swung wide and a tall silver-haired woman stood on the threshold. Donoghue noted the poise of a person who is, or was, well used to holding a position of authority. She eyed Donoghue curiously and, despite the fact that a strange and large man had walked down her gloomy driveway on a dark evening and had rung her doorbell, the old woman showed not the slightest sign of fear.

'Mrs McMillan?' asked Donoghue, reading the name above the letterbox and smiling so as to reassure the lady that she need have no fear, though he doubted that she needed the reassurance.

'Miss McMillan,' replied the woman firmly.

'I'm sorry. Police, Miss McMillan.' Donoghue showed her his ID. 'We think you may be of some assistance to us. May I come in?'

'I thought you might be a policeman,' said the woman, stepping aside. 'I've noticed the activity across the road. I presume that's what you've come about?' She shut the front door behind Donoghue and indicated an open door on the left of the hallway. Donoghue walked into the room. It was large, with solid pieces of furniture. From the little he had seen of the house it seemed a well-

ordered home, contradicting the impression given by the
outside of the house. He thought that, as her years
advanced, Miss McMillan had retreated from the garden
but had managed to retain control over the inside of the
house. She asked Donoghue to take a seat.

'You're right, it is about the incident across the road,'
he said, sinking into an armchair. It was a comfortable
chair, but nothing like the chesterfields that had been
enjoyed by Miss Pahl. 'I wonder if you could tell us
anything about the lady who lived there?'

'Lived? Is she dead? I saw the stretcher being carried to
an ambulance.'

'Yes, she is. She died in suspicious circumstances.'

'Murdered?'

'Probably. Do you mind if I smoke?'

'No, not at all. Some tea, perhaps?'

'Thank you, no,' replied Donoghue, taking his pipe
from his pocket. 'We know very little about the lady who
lived opposite. Anything you can tell us would be helpful,
Miss McMillan.'

Miss McMillan sat in the chair adjacent to Donoghue.
She thought he was most unlike a policeman. His
manner, his dress, put her in mind of a bank manager.
'Well,' she said, 'I don't know whether I can be of any
help; I'm sorry, your name?'

'Donoghue.'

'I don't know if I can help you, Mr Donoghue. I dare
say you approached my house because it looked like the
sort of house in which a nosy old spinster would live, but
really I keep myself to myself. So did Miss Pahl. I rarely
saw her. Sometimes I would only know if she was in
because the lights would be burning in the evening. She
had a car, a little silver one, but she always kept it in the
garage at the side of her house. It was never left in the
street or the driveway, not even for ten minutes. At least,
I never saw it parked outside.'

'How long had she had the car? Wasn't it fairly new?'

'Oh, she got it on the first of August this year, when the new numbers came out, you see.'

That was true. For someone who kept herself to herself Miss McMillan was beginning to look to Donoghue like a promising source of information.

'Did she have many visitors?'

'Hardly any. You say she was murdered. How was she murdered?'

'I'd rather not say if you don't mind.'

'Oh my.'

'Visitors, Miss McMillan?'

'Oh yes, hardly any. Sometimes she seemed to have an overnight guest. I'd usually know when she was having an overnight guest by the postman.'

'The postman?'

'The postman rarely called at her house. I really do keep myself to myself, Mr Donoghue, but some things one can't help noticing. Well, when the postman did call she usually had a guest arrive two or three days later.'

'What sort of guest?'

'All men. But I don't think anything improper went on. You can tell by the lights.'

'What sort of men? Young? Old?'

'Mostly quite young, but men rather than boys. They seemed to be in their thirties. Not unlike yourself, Mr Donoghue.'

Donoghue was forty-one. He let the compliment pass.

'How did they arrive, Miss McMillan?' He began to take notes.

'I didn't see all of them arrive, but those I did see were brought by Miss Pahl in her car. She also took them away again the morning after they arrived.'

'How often did she have such visitors?'

'About once a month. Usually a week before the little van arrived.'

'The van?'

'A small yellow one. It came once a month. The last Friday of each month, in fact. It was there some days ago.'

'Can you describe it?'

'Well, it was small and it was yellow.'

'Was there anything that could set it apart from other small yellow vans?'

'Well, there was an aerial sticking out of the roof; oh, and there was something written on the side. I remember because I know the origin of the name, it's from a Fats Waller song. I used to dance to Fats Waller in my young days, you know, "Your Feet's Too Big", "The Joint Is Jumpin'." ' She smiled to herself.

'What was on the side of the van?'

'Oh, "Sea-Food, Mama" and an address, but I could only make out Hampstead. I presumed it had something to do with the catering trade. It sounded like a swish little restaurant which specialized in fish dishes.'

'What happened when the van arrived?'

'It was driven into the garage like the car. Miss Pahl seemed to be very particular. Even though it was only there for about an hour she wouldn't allow it to remain on the driveway for even that length of time.'

'Did you see any of her visitors more than once?'

'Only one.'

'Describe him, please.'

'Oh, short, slim, dark hair, glasses. Seemed to be rich, he wore a sports jacket with a loud check.'

'Loud?'

'Bright. He had a dark complexion, well, sallow would be the better word. But then you'd expect that.'

'Why?'

'He was Chinese, Mr Donoghue. All Chinese are sallow, or haven't you noticed?'

★

Donoghue returned to Dominique Pahl's house. The constable on the door had been relieved and it was a fresh-faced young policeman who saluted Donoghue nervously. Donoghue nodded to him and entered the house. He found King in the drawing-room, sitting on one of the settees and leafing through a leather-bound notebook. He stood as Donoghue entered the room. Donoghue sat on the other settee and motioned King to sit down and then proceeded to look intently at him.

'Pretty interesting house,' said King, well used to his senior's way of staring silently when requesting information. 'It's huge, rooms everywhere, but she only seemed to use four. This one; a large bedroom with clothes, female clothes, in the wardrobe and drawers, which I reckoned was her room; a second bedroom had a made-up bed but no clothes in the furniture. I reckon it was used as a guest-room.'

'It was,' said Donoghue.

'The fourth room she used was the kitchen. She used to eat in there as well as cook, because the dining-room has a musty smell and an inch of dust on the tables and chairs. All the other rooms are full of junk or empty. Dare say the junk might reveal something but I didn't give it a close look.'

'Find anything at all?' Donoghue began to refill his pipe.

'Not a great deal. No letters or anything, but I found these two photographs. This one was in a frame,' he held up a colour photograph of a child, a girl of about three, she was standing in front of a brick wall and smiling at the camera. 'And this one was hidden behind it.' He handed the second photograph to Donoghue.

The second photograph showed six girls standing in a group on the banks of the Kelvin. They were smiling, wearing gowns and holding scrolls in their hands. Behind them was the unmistakable tower of Glasgow University. The girl on the extreme left of the group was Dominique Pahl. Donoghue turned the photograph over. On the reverse a neat hand had written 'graduation' and the names of the other five girls in the photograph.

'I expect they went and got good and drunk after this,' said Donoghue. 'This is my old alma mater. I don't remember too clearly what happened after my graduation ceremony and the hangover lasted for two days. What do you make of it?'

'Well, now we know she was at university, we could find her friends through the university records. They might tell us more about Miss Pahl.'

'Something for you to pick up tomorrow, then. What's that?' Donoghue nodded to the leather-bound notebook that King was holding.

'I don't know what to make of it.' He handed the book to Donoghue.

Donoghue leafed through the notebook. Some pages were blank, but most contained blocks of numbers. He was silent for a few moments, then he said 'Where did you find it?'

'At the back of a drawer in her bedroom.'

'What else was in the drawer?'

'Well.' King coughed. 'Her underclothes mostly.'

'Underclothes?'

'Yes.'

'Do you think that there's any significance to that?'

'I'm not sure, I can't see any.'

'Can't you? You're married, aren't you? To a charming lady, I seem to remember.'

'Yes,' said King, still puzzled.

'Where does she keep her clothes, her underclothes specifically?'

'In a drawer.'

'Separate from your clothes?'

'Yes.'

'Do you notice anything about the way she acts towards that drawer?'

'I can't say that I have, sir.'

'Does she not always ensure that it's shut? Always pushes it home more firmly than any other drawer?'

'Well, since you mention it . . .'

'It's the drawer where her most intimate things are kept, where she feels most possessive and jealous and territorial and secretive, and most offended by intrusion. So, if Ms Pahl chooses to hide a coded book in such a drawer, what then do you think is the significance?'

'That it's important to her.'

'Right. This poor woman seems to have been totally controlled by something which she was powerless to fight against. But she hid this, and the photograph of her graduation, so that it wouldn't be found by whatever was controlling her. Question is, why?'

'The first thing to do is crack the code,' said King.

'Montgomerie can do that. He's quite bright when he's not womanizing.'

'Can I ask what you found over the road, sir?'

'Yes, but I'm not telling you here. What time were you on this morning?'

'Six.'

'Tired?'

'I've got my second wind.'

'Not tired enough for a drink, then?'

They went to a small hotel on Albert Drive. The bar was modest and softly lit, the chairs were upholstered in purple velvet. The bar re-affirmed Donoghue's prejudiced Edinbrovian view that hotels were the only places in Big G where a guy can get a civilized drink and a quiet conversation. His civilized drink was a brandy-sour and he quietly conversed with King about the interview with Miss McMillan who kept herself to herself but who managed to be very observant. They bought a round each, left the bar at 11 p.m. and drove to P Division station.

Ray Sussock sat at his desk. He tore the note up and dropped the shreds into his waste-bin. It had arrived at his flat in the midday post but he hadn't read it until 11.15 p.m. In a spiky hand his wife had called him 'a selfish disagreeable old runt', but if he came back to her, she would forgive him. He remembered his wife always pronounced that word 'disagrebble' and seemed to choose words with 'k' or 't' sounds so that she could spit them at him.

He glanced out of the window. In the street lights he could make out a thin drizzle falling on Sauchiehall Street. He was fifty-four and a detective-sergeant, and suspected he had only won extended service as a reward for long service. His senior was thirteen years his junior and the detective-constables were bright boys who would make his rank before they were out of their twenties. His petition for divorce was filed, his son was a homosexual and his accommodation was a rented room in the West End.

Donoghue and King entered the room. Sussock started to stand but Donoghue waved him down.

'Telex reply came from the Netherlands Police, sir,' said Sussock. 'They have an active file on Kedderman Exports and know of Dominique Pahl, also known as Domino Pahl. They'd like to send one of their men over, otherwise they'll let us have all the information they've got.'

'What did you reply, Ray?'

'I didn't, I was waiting . . .'

'Well, get on it for Christ's sake, send a Telex immediately, we would be pleased to welcome one of their staff. And book a room for him at a good hotel.'

'Yes, sir,' Sussock stood.

'Any news from Montgomerie?'

'No, sir. He's still watching McFarlane.' Sussock left the room and walked down the corridor, looking for an empty room to make the phone-call in private. He told himself he hadn't been granted extended service for nothing, that it was more than a reward for long service, and he did have the love of WPC Willems, whose exquisitely beautiful form was at that moment lying in his bed. He found an empty office and dialled the Telex operator service. Perhaps there was something he could salvage from the mess after all?

CHAPTER 3

A young girl with nervous movements showed King into a dark oak-panelled ante-room. There was an old wooden chest on the floor with an equally ancient chair standing next to it. What small amount of light there was came through a window set high in the wall.

'Mr Wilson will be with you in a minute, sir,' said the girl, leaving the room and pulling the door shut behind her. King sat on the chair. The room was quiet, and although he had just walked down an echoing corridor from a busy office and there was a busy road outside, King could hear nothing. He stood and walked around the room just to make some noise. Mr Wilson's minute extended to three and King was about to release himself from the dungeon when a young man in a grey suit opened the door with a flourish. He had light-coloured hair and wore glasses. He extended a hand to King.

'Sorry to keep you, Mr King,' he said, smiling. 'Hope the sensory deprivation didn't get to you.'

'It was beginning to,' replied King, accepting Wilson's

hand loosely. He was not impressed by his welcome.

'I can imagine. We haven't anywhere else for our visitors to sit down. We don't get a deal of visitors in Admin and so waiting-rooms don't get a high priority rating.'

'Or maybe they don't visit because there's no waiting area,' said King, following Wilson down the corridor. Wilson had a spring in his step which King felt arose from a certain self-importance. He thought Wilson was about twenty-three.

'Doubt it, my friend,' replied Wilson without turning, but raising his voice to ensure that King heard him. 'Not many people are interested in records. My office is down here, were all the clatter is coming from.'

'Music to my ears,' said King drily.

Wilson's office was a small room set in a larger office which contained three rows of typists and walls lined with filing cabinets. The large office was decorated with posters of horses and landscapes, with jars of flowers and with battered copies of *Cosmopolitan* and *19* lying on the desk-tops. There was an incessant hammering of typewriters. A Lamb's Navy Rum calendar on the wall behind Wilson's desk proclaimed his small room as a male enclave.

'See what I mean?' asked Wilson, spreading his hand. 'Who would want to visit us? You see one office you've seen them all.'

A telephone rang on the desk next to where Wilson was standing; he ignored it, and a typist left her own desk twenty feet away and picked up the phone. 'It's for you, Mr Wilson,' said the girl, holding the receiver. Wilson took the receiver without looking at the girl. He said 'Wilson,' then, moments later, said, 'Call back in five minutes, will you.' He put the receiver back on the rest.

'Oh, I don't know,' said King. 'Each office has its own character.'

'I haven't noticed. Come into my office. How do you like your coffee?'

'Just milk, please.'

'Two coffees—no sugar, please, Liz,' Wilson yelled across the room, and the girl who had answered the phone rose again from her seat.

'So what can I do for you, Mr King?' Wilson sat behind his desk. 'I take it this is a police matter?'

'Yes.' King sat in the chair in front of Wilson's desk. Beer mats were pinned to the wall and the November girl was lying on a beach in a wet-suit. 'I want some information about a group of female students who graduated about ten years ago.'

'Do you indeed?' Wilson leaned forward and pyramided his fingers under his nose. 'What sort of information?'

'You are in charge here, are you, Mr Wilson?' said King, perturbed by Wilson's youth.

'For the next few days. The boss is away on a course, the Assistant Registrar is on holiday. I usually work in the Accounts Department, but I've come here to cover.'

'I see,' said King. 'Well, we'd like to know their present whereabouts, or at least the last known addresses.'

'You're clutching at a thin straw. Most students give their parents' address, and if these students graduated ten years ago they're likely to be anywhere except at their parents'.' Wilson smiled. He thought he'd helped King greatly.

King tried to be patient. Last Sunday evening a discussion group at the Friends Meeting House had agreed that one need not be physical to be violent. King tried not to be violent. 'Even that would give us more than we've got at the moment, Mr Wilson.'

'Even if such information could help you I'm not sure that I can release it.'

'Why?'

'Because I have an obligation to protect the confidentiality of personal information given to us by the students.'

'I can assure you it will be treated in confidence, Mr Wilson.'

'Ah.' Wilson held up a finger. 'Now supposing I told all to everybody who said that?' He smiled again. 'I haven't even seen your identification yet.'

King took out his ID and handed it to Wilson, who held it at a distance, inspecting it leisurely.

'I mean, I can't just tell anybody anything,' he said, handing back the ID.

'Supposing I told you that I just wasn't anybody?'

'Even so, I'm not sure I can release this information.'

'This is a murder enquiry, Wilson.' King felt his attitude harden. He tried to control it.

'Oh.'

King nodded.

'That's serious, isn't it?'

'Fairly. In the scale of things it falls somewhere between pissing in a close and High Treason. People have even been known to be executed for it.'

'Wrongly, sometimes, eh?' Wilson's teeth flashed. 'Not infallible, are you? Sure you've got it right this time?'

'We haven't got anything, which is why we need your help.'

There was a tap on the glass door and Liz walked into the office holding two mugs of coffee. Wilson's small room was suddenly filled with the clattering of typewriters.

'Just put them on the desk,' said Wilson.

Liz set the mugs down and left the room closing the door behind her.

'Where were we?' asked Wilson, reaching for one of the mugs.

'Nowhere.' King reckoned he wasn't going to get very

far with Wilson by negotiation. 'Listen, Wilson,' he said firmly. 'Let me lay it on the line for you. Either you give me the information we want or I'll have a warrant sworn and we'll turn your office over until we get what we want. It'll take months for you to get your filing back in shape. How long do you stay here?'

'Another three days, until the end of the week.'

'You think you can put it back together before Friday? We do a very thorough job.'

'You can't do that!'

'We can.'

'Anyway, this isn't the only register in the university. Each faculty has got one.'

'The names of the alumni are here. I checked.'

'You don't give me a lot of options.'

'I'm not trying to sell you something, Wilson. I'm not giving you any options. If you don't give it, we'll take it.'

'OK.' Wilson had paled visibly. 'What do you want to know?'

King reached into his pocket and pulled out his notebook. 'If you'd like to take these names down, Mr Wilson . . .' King read out the five names that had been written on the back of the photograph and added Dominique Pahl's name to the list. 'We'd like the addresses that you may have against these names. We believe these girls graduated together about ten years ago.'

'That's not much to go on.'

'It's all we've got.'

'What faculty were they?'

'Haven't a clue.'

'You don't know their faculty?' Wilson's voice became a whine.

'I think that's what I said.'

'It'll take hours.'

King reached forward and took hold of the second mug

that lay on Wilson's desk. 'I've got hours,' he said.

Wilson left the office angrily. King felt he had to concede one point to Wilson; he wasn't infallible, and he wondered if he could ever be a man of peace while he was a policeman.

Montgomerie knew that Donoghue was displeased, but he couldn't tell whether he was displeased with his report or with the content of the report. He only knew that when Donoghue read a report with deeply furrowing brows he was displeased. When Donoghue reached the end of the report and turned again to the beginning and started to re-read it, then Montgomerie knew he was very displeased.

'Curious,' said Donoghue finally and reached for his pipe. 'What do you make of it?'

'Hard to say, sir,' said Montgomerie. He found it hard to say because he didn't know what to make of it.

'What do you mean?'

'Well, it needs more investigation. The woman might be a fancy bit of stuff who can afford to live at the Antonine, and McFarlane's money may come from the horses and he might just happen to enjoy driving prawn vans about. But I doubt it.' Montgomerie was nervous. Despite his youth he held conservative ideals; he liked women who didn't cling and who offered simple, uncomplicated relationships, and he liked old-fashioned detective-inspectors; the sort that took their orders and gave their orders. The new breed, committed to staff development, he found a threatening species.

'What do you think is happening?' Donoghue lit his pipe with his gold-plated lighter.

'Frankly, I don't know. We need to know more about both.'

'I agree.' Donoghue grunted and pulled on his pipe. Blue smoke began to fill the office. 'Given the pressures on Superintendent Findlater to cut costs, which one should we watch? He'll never wear a surveillance of both.'

'I'd say McFarlane,' said Montgomerie. 'His lifestyle is all wrong, he sticks out like a rhino in a snake-pit. Given his money, from whatever source, the woman may well be a legitimate conquest.'

'I agree. It reminds me of the Inverness corruption case some years ago. We first got suspicious about a councillor when his wife was seen in the local supermarket wearing a mink coat and with her hair in curlers.'

Montgomerie smiled.

'But, that aside, how do we find out more about McFarlane? You indicate in your report that we have no prior knowledge of him.'

'No. I've checked our files and also the Police National Computer. There are one or two Donald McFarlanes, of course, but none of them is our man.' Montgomerie cleared his throat. 'We could go over his flat.'

'Bit drastic, isn't it?'

'Well . . .'

'Try to be more like a fox and less like a bull elephant. Let's sniff around our quarry before we pounce. If you charge in you'll just put him to flight. Remember that time is your greatest friend; usually, anyway.'

Montgomerie looked puzzled. Donoghue continued, 'What can we find out about McFarlane without turning his flat upside down?'

'Well,' said Montgomerie. 'We can check the length of his stay at Hyndland Crescent and how long he's been running the Granada.'

'That's right, and anything else that can help us build a picture of the man without alerting him to our interest. That should keep you busy for the rest of the afternoon. Have you been able to have a look at the code-book yet, the one we found among Dominique Pahl's knickers?'

'No, I . . .'

'Perhaps you can do it while you're phoning round.
What are you doing this evening? You might take it
home. I find I do a lot of good work by lamplight.'

'I was hoping to go out this evening, sir.'

'I dare say she'll keep.'

Montgomerie rose from the chair, swearing softly.

'Your report,' said Donoghue. He handed
Montgomerie a sheet of paper. 'Well, it's all there, but
have a look at it and see how you can improve it. Put
yourself into it, give it a voice. This is a profession, and I
see no reason why CID officers shouldn't record their
analysis and opinions as well as straight facts.'

'I'll have a look at it,' said Montgomerie, clutching the
sheet of paper.

'Let me have it back by tomorrow morning. Oh, by the
way, at five p.m., or thereabouts, one Inspector Van der
Veeght of the Royal Netherlands Police Force will be
arriving at the airport. Abbotsinch, that is. Will you go to
meet him?'

'I was hoping to get off at two, sir.'

'If you wanted to punch a time-card you should have
taken a job in a factory. Instead, you chose to enter a
profession and you took on responsibilities. Just meet the
inspector from the five o'clock flight and take him directly
to his hotel. Ray Sussock had booked him into the North
British but I changed it this morning.'

'Where is it now?'

'Oddly enough it's the Antonine. Don't ever think that
your reports are completely without influence. I'll be in
the bar at five-thirty. Perhaps you'll help me welcome the
inspector before you go home and study Dominique
Pahl's coded book?'

'I'd be delighted,' said Montgomerie drily.

The plane was a British Airways Trident. It dropped
down from the low clouds in a nose-up attitude and

slightly skewed, leaving a brown vapour trail which hung over the river. Montgomerie turned away from the window and left the observation lounge to make his way to the main concourse. He was tired; he'd got home at 1 a.m. after leaving his observation outside McFarlane's flat, slept for five hours and was back on duty at 6 a.m. Now it was 5.30 p.m. and he was still on duty, and no amount of Airport Authority coffee had been able to prevent his eyelids from feeling like two lumps of lead.

Inquiring into the life of Donald McFarlane had taken Montgomerie only two phone calls. National Police Computer had been able to inform him that DMF 1000, Granada, Black, was registered to Donald McFarlane and had been purchased new eighteen months previously. It had replaced an older Morris which had also carried McFarlane's personalized number plate. The address on his licence was 197 Hyndland Crescent, he had two endorsements for speeding, and according to his licence he was twenty-five years old. The Rates section of Strathclyde Regional Council took down his request for information, noted his name and designation and called him back. Donald McFarlane had been the owner of 197 Hyndland Cresent for the last eighteen months.

Montgomerie worked methodically, one stage at a time, with a freshly made cup of coffee to start each stage. He wrote up his findings about Donald McFarlane, made a cup of coffee and began to rewrite his report of the surveillance of McFarlane, first written at 8 a.m. that morning. He added more, put himself into it, recorded his considered professional opinion that Donald McFarlane was acting in a manner which warranted further investigation. He put the rewrite in Donoghue's pigeonhole and made another cup of coffee. Then he phoned Fiona.

'I told you not to phone me at work, Mal,' she complained when Montgomerie had identified himself. 'I just haven't the time to stop and chat, and anyway, it's not particularly private.'

'Couldn't phone you any other time.' He could picture her standing there with one hand thrust deep into the pocket of her smock and with that rubber-tubed thing round her neck.

'You could have phoned from home. Don't you get off in quarter of an hour? It's always quieter mid-afternoon.'

'Some chance of me getting off on time,' he said. 'That's what I'm phoning about. I don't know whether I'll be able to make it tonight.'

'Malcolm!'

'I'm sorry, I'm going Dutch.'

'Going Dutch! With whom?'

'Inspector Donoghue, also known as Fabian. Heap big chief.'

'Where are you going?'

'To meet the Flying Dutchman.'

'You've been drinking!'

'Instant coffee. Milk, no sugar. Three cups in the last hour.'

'You'll still rot your insides. So you're not coming over tonight?'

'I'm going drinking.'

'Malcolm, this is a relationship we have, you know.'

'I know.'

'I don't think you are taking it seriously.'

'I am. Listen, the good Inspector has invited me to entertain a bloody Dutchman who's coming to help us out with a murder enquiry. I'm meeting him at the airport and taking him to the Antonine and me and Fabian are going to do the entertaining.'

'I see.' There was a note of relief in her voice. 'That's fine, thanks for telling me. Do you think you'll be able to get over later?'

'Don't know. Depends what he's like. If he drinks like a

fish I probably won't be.'

'Well, how about I go round to your flat and prepare something for when you do come in?'

'Smashin'. Get some wine and expect me when you see me.' He replaced the receiver. He reckoned Fiona was OK.

The rear wheels of the Trident touched the runway, and moments later the nose wheel also sank on to the tarmac. The roar of the engines in reverse thrust rolled across the airport as Montgomerie arrived on the main concourse and stood watching the disembarkation gate.

Van der Veeght was a heavily built man, as tall as Donoghue and as broad as a Dutch barge. He had blond hair and a round face, and wore a light-blue polyester suit with highly polished black shoes. Montgomerie thought he was in his late thirties, and he could tell by the way Van der Veeght stood, balanced very slightly forward, that the Dutchman was not only large but that he was very fit into the bargain. Montgomerie approached him because he looked Dutch, and looked like a policeman. He was also the only person among the passengers on the flight from Schiphol who stood on the main concourse with a raincoat folded over his arm and a pair of matching suitcases on the floor beside him, looking as though he was waiting for someone to meet him.

'Excuse me, sir,' said Montgomerie cautiously. 'Inspector Van der Veeght?'

'Ja!' There was a flash of white teeth and Montgomerie's hand was snatched and crushed in Van der Veeght's grip.

'Is this your first visit to Scotland, Inspector?' asked Montgomerie as they drove into the city. He asked out of courtesy, he was feeling too tired to be interested.

'Yes, it is, Malcolm, but before I have been in England

and also in Ireland. With my wife two years ago we visited
Dorset and also the Island of Wight. And you, Malcolm,
have you visited Holland?'

'I was in Amsterdam a few years ago.'

'This is certainly a splendid-looking city, Malcolm.'
Van der Veeght looked around him with obvious interest
as Montgomerie drove over the Kingston bridge. 'So
modern, so huge. It reminds me of New York, with the
river and the tall buildings; it is violent, too, like New
York, isn't it, Malcolm?'

'Not a bit of it, Inspector.' Montgomerie shook his
head. 'It's not as black as it's painted.'

'It has such a name, such a — a — reputation.'

'You're in what is probably the safest city in Europe,
Inspector. Glasgow streets are as safe as anywhere. If you
want a punch-up, this city will give you all you can
handle, but if you don't look for trouble you'll be left
alone. You can't say that about London.'

'You cannot say it about Amsterdam,' conceded Van
der Veeght, still looking intently around him.

'It's a good city,' said Montgomerie. 'The reputation
for violence comes from the gangs who give each other
tankings; there's also sectarian tension, but we don't get a
lot of muggings, and tourists usually pass through without
any trouble.'

Montgomerie came off the motorway at Charing Cross
and drove up Sauchiehall Street, on to Bath Street, down
past Queen Street station, on to George Street and into
Ingram Street. He found a parking space across the road
from the entrance to the Antonine. Van der Veeght
insisted on carrying his own suitcases into the hotel. They
were both heavy; Montgomerie could see the handle
fastenings straining under the weight; but they were lifted
smoothly like two half-full bags of groceries. Van der
Veeght checked into the hotel and he and Montgomerie
walked to the bar, leaving a porter to wrestle the

Dutchman's luggage towards the lift.

Donoghue and Van der Veeght sipped brandy, and Montgomerie took a lager but limited it to a half-pint measure. They sat around a low circular table in the corner of the bar, Donoghue and Van der Veeght leaning forward engaged in conversation, with Montgomerie sitting back, speaking when spoken to, as protocol and his position in the hierarchy dictated. He was pleased Fiona had suggested she should go round to his flat; he had something to look forward to.

'So will you tell me or will I tell you?' grinned Van der Veeght.

Donoghue smiled. 'I don't think there's much to tell, Heer Van der Veeght.'

'You may call me Jan.'

'Jan, I don't think—'

'And what will I call you, Scotchman?'

'Inspector, if you don't mind,' said Donoghue.'

Montgomerie managed to keep from smiling.

'You are too frigid,' said Van der Veeght. 'Too frigid, then I too must remain Heer Van der Veeght.' He sat back in his chair.

'As you wish,' said Donoghue. 'Well—' he sipped his brandy—'it really started early Sunday morning, very early, when Dominique Pahl walked into the police station, got as far as giving her name and asking for protection and then walked away again. We found her body on Monday morning. She'd been murdered.'

'Filled full of heroin?' asked Van der Veeght, still sitting back in his chair.

'How did you know?'

'I know. She took the sensible decision, believe me.'

'Earlier in the day we had discovered that heroin, good quality stuff, worth about three hundred thousand pounds, had turned up in restaurants across the Central Belt.'

'The Central Belt?'

'The plain in Central Scotland,' Donoghue stammered. Van der Veeght's question had interrupted his flow. He felt the Dutchman had done it deliberately. 'The area between Edinburgh and Glasgow; has towns such as Falkirk and Cumbernauld.'

'So. Proceed.' The Dutchman waved his hand.

'Well, we traced the source to a shoestring and sealing-wax operation called Scot Euro Imports, who in turn import from Kedderman Exports of Rotterdam. Once a month Scot Euro Imports receives a batch of prawns which have a red label on the boxes. These they set aside for collection by Ms Pahl.'

'Now deceased,' said Van der Veeght.'

'The very same. The prawns were later collected by a van with the name of a chic-sounding London restaurant printed on the side. We've informed the Metropolitan Police and they are watching the place.'

'Good,' said the Dutchman. Donoghue detected a trace of cynicism in his voice.

'We were suspicious of one of the employees of Scot Euro Imports and so one of our men watched him. Montgomerie here, in fact.'

'Yes.' Montgomerie sat forward; he was thinking of Fiona, of her body and his fingers running over her flesh. He nearly missed his cue. 'Yes. He seems to lead a double life. Van-lad in the daytime and young blade about town after sundown. Picked a lady up last night and took her back to his flat, she was all furs and glistening stones. She stays at this hotel, as a matter of fact.'

Van der Veeght's eyes met Donoghue's, and after a short stony stare the Dutchman's face cracked into a wide grin. Donoghue also smiled.

'That's basically all we know,' said Donoghue. 'It's all written up in a file which will be made available to you.' He raised his hand imperiously and summoned the waiter.

Donoghue and Van der Veeght talked about the flight until the second round of drinks had been laid on the table, for which Montgomerie suddenly realized he was expected to pay. Again. When the waiter had gone, Donoghue changed the subject. 'You said you had information about Dominique Pahl.'

'Not a great deal. We don't know any of her history.'

'We're working on that,' said Donoghue.

'So. Even so, we knew her as Domino Pahl, and she was one of a lot of runners, the carrier pigeons who ferry narcotics. You would think for the risks they run they would be high in the organization, not so.' He shook his head. 'They are little fish, often even addicts themselves. We net them frequently, but they will never give us any information about the organization. Domino Pahl worked for an organization which had a legitimate front as an export agency, Kedderman Exports, you have traced back so far already.' He sipped his brandy. 'Kedderman Exports is run by a Triad, an oriental organization, probably Malaysian in origin; there is no "top man" but an inner council of three. They've been exporting heroin to all parts of Europe for the last twenty years.'

'And you've never had any evidence?'

'None.' The Dutchman's manner had grown warmer. Donoghue was pleased. 'Not for the inner council, we don't even know their names. We've tried to infiltrate, but we always find our men in the Ijsselmeer. Usually tortured before death. We catch the little ones from time to time, like Domino Pahl, but they never tell us anything. It is usually because the Triad has some hold over them against which even death is a pleasant alternative.'

'What in God's name is it?'

'Who knows?' Van der Veeght shrugged his shoulders. 'In each case it is different; it depends on the weakness of the individual, or perhaps I mean vulnerable.'

'Vulnerability,' said Donoghue. 'So that's what you meant when you said Dominique Pahl took the sensible alternative?'

'Yes. A shot of heroin is the common form of execution. It is painless and quick. Miss Pahl must have preferred it to whatever her alternative was to be — perhaps even having her stomach burst by the water torture.'

'What!'

'One of my detectives whom we found in the weeds on the banks of the Ijsselmeer had had his stomach burst. The medical men said that he was alive when the water which was being forced down his throat burst through his stomach.'

'Good God!' Donoghue grimaced.

'Ja. Even the strong feel weak. Do not be ashamed. We know the Triad made a public show of such things, the French have an expression . . .'

'*Pour encourager les autres*,' said Montgomerie.

'So,' said the Dutchman, nodding at Montgomerie. 'Faced with such an alternative I think I too would roll up my sleeve.'

'Just for losing twelve sachets of heroin,' Montgomerie mumbled.

'Do you think the bastard who did this is still around, Heer Van der Veeght?' asked Donoghue.

'Yes, I think so,' replied the Dutchman. 'Domino Pahl may have been just a little fish but she will leave a big hole. Have you searched her house?'

'Not thoroughly yet. But we did find a photograph and a notebook.'

'What's in the notebook?' asked Van der Veeght.

'We don't know.' Donoghue raised his eyebrows and looked at Montgomerie.

'It's in code,' said Montgomerie hastily. 'I'm working on it.'

'I would like to see the house, Inspector,' said Van der Veeght.

'I was hoping that the Dutch businessman might ingratiate himself with the lady in furs and diamonds who stays in this hotel.'

'I see,' said Van der Veeght. 'So. To whom does this Dutch businessman make his reports?'

'To me,' said Donoghue. 'I'm in charge. I am co-ordinating the operation.'

'Which is why I must call you "Inspector".'

Donoghue nodded.

'You are too cold. I do not like it, but . . .' Van der Veeght shrugged his shoulders. 'I will still want to see the house.'

'It's not very convenient just now, Inspector Van der Veeght, we're still looking at the house ourselves. I really think McFarlane's girl-friend would prove a more fruitful line of inquiry.'

'I am being restricted,' complained Van der Veeght.

'Not at all, but this is a team approach. I think your talents are best put to use in this hotel. If, however, you come across a good reason to visit the house, please don't hesitate to ask me. But you understand, Inspector Van der Veeght, I must know the movements of everyone in the team.'

'I still think you are restricting me, Scotchman. But I will buy you a brandy.' He raised his hand. 'You too, Malcolm.'

CHAPTER 4

Wilson handed King a sheet of paper, on which were listed six addresses, one against each of the names King had given Wilson.

'It didn't take hours after all,' said King, reading over the list. 'One hour fifteen minutes, in fact. Thank you.'

'It took long enough.' Wilson sat back in his chair. He had paled a little since King's arrival. 'I'm behind with the monthly stats. return now.'

'You'll catch up.' King stood and folded the sheet of paper and slipped it in his notebook. He put the notebook in his jacket pocket.

'Would you really have used a warrant to search the office?' asked Wilson meekly.

'Oh, I doubt it,' said King turning to the door and the clatter of typewriters. 'So thanks for your co-operation, Mr Wilson, I'll mention it to my governor.'

'I'd rather you didn't,' replied Wilson.

King sat in his car and gave the list a closer scrutiny. Like most of the students at Glasgow's two universities, the six girls had all been natives of the city, and they had all graduated from the History Faculty eleven years previously. Dominique Pahl's home address eleven years ago was given as 19 Ram Street, Shettleston. King tossed the list on to the passenger seat and drove across the city to Shettleston. Ram Street was still located on the street map of the city, but the street itself had fundamentally changed. Only one house remained, on the corner, with the name of the street bolted on to the masonry. The rest of the 116 houses had been pulled down and in their place were grassy knolls and young saplings. King drove to the next nearest address.

27 Duntarvie Quad was a solid sandstone tenement just off Shettleston Road. The stair was clean and smelled of disinfectant, the decorative tiles were still intact; it was a good stair, a wally close. The McLeans' lived two up. Their door was solid and darkly stained, with their name painted on a tartan background and screwed to the door at eye-level. The door handle and letterbox were made of brass and were highly polished. King pressed the doorbell

which, to his amusement, rang the Westminster chimes. The door opened about thirty seconds later. It was swung open and held wide by a stout woman who looked to be in her mid-sixties. Her hair was silver and she smiled confidently at King. He felt it was strange to find someone who would swing her door wide at an unexpected ringing of her bell. But then, Number 27 was a good stair, waiting only for a housebreaking or a solvent-sniffers' gathering in the close mouth before all the residents had peep-holes and safety-chains fitted to their doors. From what King could see, the McLeans' flat was cluttered but not untidy. 'Police,' he said.

The woman stopped smiling.

'Mrs McLean?' asked King.

The woman nodded.

'We're trying to locate your daughter Tracy, Mrs McLean.'

'Do you have identification?'

King showed his ID. 'She's not in any trouble, Mrs McLean, but we think she may be able to give us some information about one of her university friends.'

'I see. I don't think she'll be able to help you and I'm certain that she's in no trouble. Tracy died five years ago.'

King's jaw dropped slightly, 'I'm . . .'

'Good day, Mr King.' The McLeans' door shut quietly but firmly. King stood on the stair and felt the disinfectant hurting his eyes. He started down towards the street. A woman was climbing the stair with a bulging shopping-bag in each hand. King stepped aside and smiled at her: he felt he had to salvage something from his visit.

The next nearest address was in G 12. King drove back across the city to the West End and parked outside 95 Queens Gardens. 95 Queens Gardens was a large house nestling in an avenue in Dowanhill. It wasn't out of place in the pocket of affluence wedged into the south-western

corner of the Byres Road/Great Western Road inter-
section. The door of 95 was a yellow-painted lightweight
frame with only one lock. King reckoned the reason the
resident didn't fear a break-in was the presence of a large
dog, which began to bark and scratch the floor before
King had even pressed the doorbell. He wondered if he
need press the bell at all with the dog making so much
racket, but he decided he ought to announce his presence
legitimately. The bell turned out to be a rough-sounding
buzzer. The wealthier you are, it seemed to King, the less
pretentious you get. The dog seemed to be working itself
into a fit, and still the door remained unanswered. King
waited. The wind blew the leaves in small whirlwinds, the
sky was grey and the clouds moved swiftly over the city.
An AA patrol cruised the street searching for a stranded
motorist. King pressed the buzzer again. He heard
another sound from behind the door, a scuffling, a rough
male voice yelling 'shut up'. The dog began to whimper
and then growl. The door was jerked open and a tall man
with a large stomach and greying hair held back a
snarling alsatian by a chain round the dog's neck. The
man looked at King. He had small eyes.

'Police,' said King.'

'Now what is it?'

King thought the man and the dog suited each other:
both snarling in unison.

'I understand you have a daughter, Mr Mathieson?'

'I've three.'

'I'm trying to trace Margaret.'

'I ought to ask you why, but as she's not my daughter
any more I don't care. I'm not interested.'

King had the awful feeling that Margaret Mathieson was
also dead. The history alumni of Glasgow University
didn't seem to have a long life expectancy. King said 'I
don't understand.'

'Don't you? It's simple. I once had four daughters. Now

I've got three. Do you understand now?'

'No,' said King calmly. First lesson in handling aggression; do not respond to it. Second lesson: avoid eye contact. King glanced up the road; the AA van had stopped next to a red car, the patrolman was burrowing in the car's engine. A woman in a green coat stood next to him, tapping her foot.

'You don't understand?'

King shook his head.

'You want me to spell it out for you?'

'If you wouldn't mind,' said King icily.

'I built a business. I came up from Bridgeton and nobody helped me. I clawed my way up. I had a wife, she's no longer around, and four daughters. I gave them all sensible names, Orange names, so nobody could mistake them for fucking Papes. I send them to the Academy, all four, three marry Orangemen, but the fourth, she had to go to the University. If that isn't enough she stabs me in the back, she goes Green, Margaret, she goes and marries a fucking Tim. I haven't got a girl called Margaret. Not any more.'

'Do you know where she lives?'

'No. I've no wish to know.'

'Do you know how I can get in contact with her?'

'Try asking for Mrs O'Neill at St Joseph's school. That's if she's still teaching. She's probably pregnant by now, they breed like rabbits, the Tims.'

The alsatian snarled, the door was slammed shut.

Orange and Green. Prods and Tims. It seemed to King that Glasgow was like two glaciers grating against each other. He drove round the corner and stopped at a telephone kiosk. One of the nice things about G 12, for those who can afford to stay there, is that the telephones don't get smashed up and a directory can last for about three months before being ripped off or ripped up. King checked for St Joseph's in the directory: it was in

Easterhouse, G 34.

He took the motorway through the city, leaving it at
the Westerhouse Road exit ramp. He drove through
Easterhouse to St Joseph's. Easterhouse was a sprawling
council housing scheme. It had four bars, one small
shopping centre, and a population greater than the city
of Perth. It was a comparatively new scheme, yet most of
the houses were rotten with damp.

King parked his car in the staff car-park of St Joseph's.
He walked into the school and stood in the foyer. He had
arrived during the lunch-break. The children eyed him,
looking sideways at him. The street-wise ones' said 'Polis!'
A woman in a gymslip, carrying a hockey stick,
approached him.

'Can I help you?' she said. She had a cold stare and legs
like oaks. She held the hockey stick across her front,
gripping it with whitening knuckles. King said he was
looking for Margaret O'Neill.

'Who are you?'

'Police.' He showed her his ID.

The woman stared at him. She didn't relax her tone.
Then she said, 'this way.'

She led King down a corridor with brown parquet floor
and yellow walls. Children milled in groups, looking at
King, the stranger, the instantly recognizable polis. The
woman bounded up a flight of stairs and King found that
he was able to keep pace with her, but not without effort.
She strode along another corridor and opened a door.
'Wait here, please,' she said.

King waited in the corridor. There were pictures on the
wall, the odd child walked by. Margaret O'Neill stepped
out of the staff-room.

'Yes?' she said. She seemed to be in her early thirties,
sensible shoes, modest grey skirt, brown pullover, short
black hair. A crucifix hung around her neck on a pale
silver chain. She had a mole on her left cheek.

'Police,' said King. 'Is there somewhere we can talk?'

'What's the trouble?' Margaret O'Neill flushed. 'What's happened?'

'The trouble is big and a lot has happened, but you've no cause to be alarmed.' King found himself smiling, something he rarely did when inquiring, but he was taken with Margaret O'Neill, so feminine, but also strong-willed, standing up to her father on every issue, rejecting the business community for teaching in a comprehensive, rejecting Protestantism for a Catholic husband, and also, it seemed, taking the faith herself. 'Is there somewhere we can talk?' he asked again, but this time without the smile.

'Yes, yes, the form-rooms are all free for the next half-hour, if that's long enough. The nearest one is just across here.'

She led King diagonally across the corridor to a classroom, rows of ink-stained desks, a blackboard, chalk-dust in the air and posters on the wall. King thought things hadn't changed much since his day, but then, since he was only twenty-five, his day wasn't that long ago. Margaret O'Neill made for the teacher's chair and sat in it without thinking, then, realizing King had nowhere to sit, sprang to her feet. King waved her down. 'Please,' he said. He leaned against one of the desks in front of Mrs O'Neill, not so near as to threaten and cow her, not so far away as to make her have to shout.

'Your father told me where to find you,' said King. 'We traced your home address through the University records.'

'My father.' Margaret O'Neill smiled. 'He's not as bad as you might have thought, he never writes, but he knows exactly where I am. He probably gave you this address because he didn't want to give my home address.'

'I see.' King took out his notebook. 'He certainly has a frightening dog, but I'll take your word for it.'

'Rusty? Yes, he's vicious, Father uses him to guard the

yard. He had a road haulage company, huge Swedish lorries.'

'Well, Mrs O'Neill,' said King, 'we're making inquiries about an old university friend of yours, Dominique Pahl.'

'Domino?' Margaret O'Neill's eyes widened. 'I haven't heard of her for years. She's not in any trouble?'

'No. Not any more. I'm afraid she's dead, Mrs O'Neill.'

Margaret O'Neill's head sagged forward. 'Sweet Jesus,' she said.

King allowed her a moment's silence and then asked: 'When did you last hear from her?'

'What? Oh, years ago, must have been four years ago. How did she die?' She raised her head.

'She was murdered.'

'Oh my God.' Again Margaret O'Neill lowered her head.

'We hardly know anything about her, Mrs O'Neill; anything you could tell us would be useful.'

'Like what, Officer? I don't know a deal myself. When did she die?'

'This last weekend. Two or three days ago.'

'Where was she living?'

'In the city. South of the river.'

'Still in the city. How was she murdered?'

'She was poisoned. I'd rather not say any more than that, Mrs O'Neill.'

'I understand. What is it you want to know?'

'Anything you could tell us would be helpful.'

'I don't know a lot, like I said. We really only knew each other for a year, our final year. I met her through another friend, Tracy McLean, she used to travel between Shettleston and the University with Domino every day for three years — in term-time, that is. Then Domino moved into a flat in Hillhead and I spent more time with her. Have you contacted Tracy McLean? I haven't heard of her for years, but I'm sure she could help you more than I could, even though Domino did latch on to me.'

King felt sick. It wasn't anything to do with him, and it wasn't a police matter, but did he have the right to allow someone to go on believing an old friend was still alive? And did he have the right to intrude and break the news? He couldn't decide. 'No, we haven't traced her yet,' he said, 'but you said she latched on to you?'

'Yes. I really saw her for the first time one night in our final year. She had just taken that flat in Hillhead, oh, it was awful, repulsive, a narrow bed with a hard mattress, stains all over the bath and a cooker in the hallway. We went there one night, just the two of us, and demolished a bottle of Martini. It went to both our heads, but hers mostly, and she told me her life story. I don't remember much, I didn't take all of it in, I spent a lot of time wondering why she was telling me all this. Have you ever had that happen to you, someone you hardly know takes you on one side and tells you all their problems?'

'Once or twice,' admitted King.

'Used to happen every term with me. I must have been some sort of sucker. Probably still am. I remember this instance vividly, but I don't recall much of what was said if you see what I mean. Of all the things that stay with me it's her eyes.'

'Her eyes?'

'Big, brown, round, sad eyes. A little girl's eyes, I'd never noticed them before. There, inside all that beauty, was a lost little girl.'

'What did she tell you?'

'That she had never had anybody and couldn't get anybody. She was an only child, grew up on a small-holding near a village called Plains which is near Airdrie. She didn't talk about her childhood, so it couldn't have been pleasant. By the time she got to the University both her parents were dead and she was in a bedsit in Shettleston.'

'No other friends or relatives?'

'No. Not that she told me of, anyway. That was her problem; nobody in her past, nobody in her present. She couldn't give of herself because she had never been given to; she always presented as being cold and distant, so, despite all the glamour, she never had a boy-friend. I suppose you could say she was "uptight". That's a word that was in vogue at the time. You were either "laid back" or "screwed up" or "uptight". Some of us read psychology as an option, we'd write essays about the infinite conditions of the psyche, but at night in the bar we'd dismiss all those we knew into one of three categories. I think I was usually "laid back", but that doesn't have any sexual implication.'

'I'm sure it doesn't,' said King.

'In fact, I only looked as though I was "laid back" and had it all together. Really I was pretty screwed up. I was breaking from home at that time.'

'I can imagine the difficulty,' said King.

'Yes. Well, it's done now. But Domino, well I really can't think of anything else to tell you about her personality. I couldn't tell her why she hadn't got any friends because I couldn't seem to communicate with her. She just could not make relationships. That night ended with her sobbing into her knees at one end of the bed and with me draped over the frame at the other end with my head spinning and an empty bottle lying between us. It wasn't like that every night; for me, anyway, Mr King.'

'I'm sure it wasn't.'

'After graduating we went our separate ways. Of all the people you meet at University you only retain contact with a handful — weird — and then a stranger comes to your door and tells you one that you didn't keep up contact with has died. At first it brings you closer to life, makes you more appreciative. But I think the guilt feelings will set in tonight.'

'Why guilt feelings?'

'I think I'd have them anyway, but especially about Domino. Somehow I think I meant a lot to her; she was trying to give to me, trying to reach out, but I was busying myself with my life, I didn't notice. No, I did notice but I pretended not to because the truth was I was a bit frightened, or maybe I just didn't care.'

'Frightened?'

'Well, I was frightened because I couldn't give to her the way she wanted to be given to. She wanted to be warmed, mothered if you like; I didn't know how to handle that sort of situation so I just shyed off and pretended not to notice. But even so I didn't realize how important I was to her until years later. Suddenly out of the blue I got a letter from her. She'd met this guy and they were getting married. I could tell by the tone of her letter that she was telling only me.'

'I'm beginning to see her,' said King.

'Are you? Can you see her? She suddenly pounces on me at University as the one to whom she will tell all her problems, and even though we were never close it was still me, a lot of years and no contact later, that she wrote to tell her good news. While I had all but forgotten her, in her mind I was as large as life, a daily influence. I think my guilt is going to be great, Mr King.'

King felt it was little use telling Margaret O'Neill that she ought not to blame herself. 'Can you remember anything about the man she was marrying?' he asked softly.

'He was a Dutchman. He lived in Amsterdam; near there, anyway, at a place called Sloten. I remember that quite well because she sent a map with her letter and an invitation to visit. Sloten lies between Schiphol Airport and Amsterdam city and we agreed, me and my husband that is, we agreed that we'd stop off and see her if ever we

visited Holland. We never got round to going. His name
was Frans Bakhuis and he ran a second-hand bookshop,
or so she said in her letter.'

King scribbled in his notebook.

'I replied and said how happy I was that she'd found
someone and sent a card that Christmas. There was no
more word from her and we never visited because we were
so hard-up; in fact, in those days we were permanently
broke. Well, some years after that she wrote and said she
had a baby, a girl; that was three years ago, more or less.
Again it was me she had to write to.'

'More or less? It's important.'

'Oh. Well, I got the letter just before our holiday in
Cornwall, and we left as the school broke up for summer.
So I received the letter in June, three years ago.'

'And the child had just been born?'

'Well, a woman who has just given birth tends to have
more important things on her mind than writing letters,
even Domino.' Margaret O'Neill smiled. 'I can't remember
the birth date but I think she wrote to me about two weeks
after the event.'

King nodded and scribbled in his book. 'There's
nothing else you can remember?'

'No, I don't think so.'

'Or about her husband and daughter?'

'Only that she called her daughter Dominique after
herself.'

'So her daughter was registered as Dominique
Bakhuis?'

'Well, I presume so, Mr King. You know as much as I
do now.'

'Yes, thank you, you've been very helpful. You don't
know whether Miss Pahl kept in touch with any other of
her university friends? Or any other person, for that
matter?'

'No, I don't. I think I was closer to her than anybody

and that was pretty distant. But like I said, you could try
Tracy McLean, if she's still in the city, that is. Myself and
Domino and Tracy and some other girls in our faculty
had our photos taken on the lawn outside the Art Gallery,
in our gowns, you know. After the photograph was taken
we went to get changed and that was literally the last time
I saw Tracy.'

'Mrs O'Neill,' said King quietly. 'This is really none of
my business and I'm not speaking as a policeman now,
but I'm afraid that this morning I found out that Tracy
McLean had also died. Five years ago. I'm sorry. I don't
know any details and there's no connection with
Dominique Pahl.'

Margaret O'Neill didn't react. She sat quite still and
stared at King. Then she said, 'Thank you for telling me.'

She remained seated, and King walked softly out of the
room, closing the door gently behind him. He walked
down the corridor and then turned as he heard a door
open behind him. Margaret O'Neill stood there.

'I remember,' she said. 'Domino's husband; she said he
only had one arm.'

It was Tuesday. 1.23 p.m.

Tuesday: 8.05 p.m.

Donoghue, Van der Veeght and Montgomerie had
stopped drinking, moved from their table in the corner of
the Antonine bar at 6.30, and taken up different
positions. Van der Veeght sat in the foyer of the hotel
reading a copy of the *International Herald Tribune* and
smoking a cigar. He was tired and he wanted to get his
head down, but the boss had insisted on work. Van der
Veeght knew that Montgomerie too wanted to get away,
to meet his girl; instead he was in the foyer, sitting
adjacent to Van der Veeght, leafing through a copy of
Scottish Field. When McFarlane entered the foyer
Montgomerie was to put down the magazine and leave

the hotel. From then on it was up to Van der Veeght to play it as he thought best. If McFarlane hadn't shown by 10 p.m. they were to call it a day.

Donoghue had caught the 7 p.m. shuttle to Edinburgh. The first-class was nearly empty, and as the train sped swiftly through Lenzie he took off his shoes and put his feet up on the opposite seat. He pulled on his pipe and opened the *Scotsman* for the first time that day. He was looking forward to getting back to his home in what he believed to be the most beautiful city in Europe, to his wife and two beautiful children. He thought rank had its privileges.

McFarlane entered the Antonine at 8.45. He walked to the reception desk and spoke to the girl, who lifted the telephone and talked into the mouthpiece. Montgomerie tossed his magazine on to the coffee-table, stretched his arms, yawned and walked slowly out of the foyer. Van der Veeght lowered his paper and was amused to see Montgomerie increase his pace once he was past the foyer, push through the revolving doors, glance at his watch and hail a taxi. Van der Veeght stopped smiling and turned his attention to McFarlane. McFarlane was standing with his back to the reception desk, surveying the foyer. His eyes briefly met Van der Veeght's and moved on unhurriedly without a trace of fear or guilt. Van der Veeght noted that McFarlane was well composed, was well groomed, with a tailored grey suit, and he also noted he was short but stocky. He stood, leaving the paper on his seat, walked over to the reception desk and stood next to McFarlane, flicking through the postcards of Glasgow and West Scotland. Once closer to McFarlane he noted an almost overpowering smell of aftershave.

The woman stepped out of the lift and crossed the foyer. McFarlane stepped forward and Van der Veeght turned and allowed himself a brief glance. There had been no exaggeration on Montgomerie's part: she walked elegantly, swathed in fur, weighed down by rocks, black hair, dark complexion, dark glasses. Van der Veeght turned back to the counter and lured the receptionist away from the keyboard by waving two postcards of Clyde paddle-steamers and tapping a fifty-pence piece on the counter. McFarlane's woman dropped her key on to the reception desk; the receptionist, attending to Van der Veeght, let it lie there. Attached to the key was a red plastic tab on which, engraved and painted in white, was the number 235.

'*Dank*,' said Van der Veeght.

Room 235 was room 35 at the end of a narrow corridor on the second floor. It was held shut by a barrel lock. There are a number of ways a locked door will yield without a key and without necessarily being kicked in. The tumblers of a regular mortise lock will fall to a gentle teasing with a bent paper-clip, and a barrel lock will give to a credit card. The card is pushed gently between the door and the frame, level with the lock, the pliable plastic will force back the spring-loaded bolt, and the door is opened with dismaying ease.

Van der Veeght shut the door behind him and slipped the credit card back into his jacket pocket. The room was in semi-darkness. A faint light came in through the curtains and a luminous dial glowed near the bed. The dominant thing about the room was the odour, the odour of scent having been laid on with a trowel until it became a smell. The woman and McFarlane seemed to Van der Veeght to be two of a kind and he wondered how they could face each other in the mornings, when the image gave way to brutal reality. He stood against the door, breathing gently, and ran his hand over the wall until he located the light switch. He shut his eyes to avoid being blinded by the sudden light and flicked the switch.

The first thing that struck him about the room when it

was exposed to the glare of harsh white light was the utter mess that it was in. It could have been struck by a whirlwind. Clothes seemed to lie everywhere; on the bed, strewn on the floor or hanging out of drawers. But it had not the stamp of a burglary; even if he had not seen the lady in furs leave the hotel a few minutes earlier, Van der Veeght would still have known it was not a burgled room because there was an order concealed in the mess. The clothes lying on the bed were at the bottom and not at the top, nothing was damaged or torn, the lamp-stand was still upright, nothing lay in the arc of the door. That it was *not* a burgled room was the striking thing: some people's rooms were constantly in such a state, but only in their homes, never their hotel rooms, where people feel less relaxed, where they do not stay long enough to create such confusion, and where chambermaids come in each day to make the bed, if nothing else.

Gently, Van der Veeght moved away from the door, frightened because the room presented problems. In a neat and ordered room it's easy to see if you have left any trace of your presence: in such a room as this, Van der Veeght knew any trace he left would be quickly camouflaged by the disarray, and might be spotted only by the resident. He knew also that it was not unknown for rooms to be deliberately made to appear in a state of disorder, when in fact the location of every pair of discarded tights had been precisely noted, and the length by which silk scarves hung from drawers had been measured to a millimetre.

Suddenly he didn't know where he was and he stopped as the fear of the unknown gripped him. Suddenly everything became aggressively alien. He thought back over his day. Kissing his wife in the departure lounge, the late autumn sun, the mid-afternoon flight to Glasgow. Glasgow? Where was Glasgow? An hour's flight from Amsterdam, across the North Sea, across Scotland.

Arriving in this city with its splendidly solid buildings, its vastness, the bustle, the sweep of new development on the river front. Now he was in a hotel room in this city. It was the same day, and the thugs were the same; this room had some connection with the monsters who killed people by forcing water down their throats until their stomachs burst and then chucked the corpses into the Ijsselmeer. But that was in Holland; this was Glasgow, Scotland.

Re-orientated, he moved forward, but he felt he should not be in the room. He sensed the room held danger, not from the room itself but from within himself. It was dangerous for him to be in the room. He was tired, culture-shocked, he'd been drinking, he was confused and his senses were dulled. He had been given no clear instructions to go into the room. No-one knew where he was, he had no support in the hotel, he had no idea how to summon assistance if he needed any. He fought against the panic he could feel rising in him, he steeled himself and moved forward, he felt he couldn't leave the room empty-handed. In a drawer by the bed he found a Dutch passport. He leafed through it. The photograph was of a woman whose hair was pinned back and who wore no glasses. But it could have been the photograph of the woman who tossed her room-key on to the reception desk. The name on the photograph was Louisa Maartens.

He thought about the way the woman had dropped the key on the reception desk. It was too cool, too casual, as if it were a lure, a bait. He backed across the room carefully and stepped into the corridor. He had the sensation of a huge net falling behind him, narrowly missing him.

CHAPTER 5

Fiona had made lasagne, and as Montgomerie burst into the flat panting his apologies she rose from the chair, kissed him and went to the kitchen. She brought his meal and laid it on the table.

'I had mine, I couldn't wait. Give me your jacket I'll hang it up for you.'

She returned to the room and sat in a deep armchair.

'We'll have to do some talking, Fiona,' said Montgomerie, with his mouth full of lasagne.

'Later. Just eat up. You're too tired. Anyway. Do you really think we need to talk to each other?' She stood and walked across the room and kissed his head. 'Eat up, big man.' She left the room. Montgomerie dug his fork into the lasagne. Big man. If anyone was big around here Montgomerie reckoned it wasn't him. He knew it had to be done tonight, it was now or never; OK, Fiona, lovely meal, but it's over, off, finished, OK? Nothing personal, but I need my freedom. Big man.

She returned to the room and placed a mug of tea beside him, crossed the room and sat on the sofa he'd recently bought from Habitat. She wore a black split-thigh skirt, 11-denier tights, high heels, white lace blouse and neatly cut black hair. He couldn't deny that she went in and out in all the right places, nor could he deny that she never nagged at him, and that the meal was waiting for him, all warmed up and succulent, and that she knew he was too knackered to enjoy wine with the meal but that a mug of tea after it was just great. He crossed the floor and sat next to her.

'Fiona . . .' he managed to say before her mouth fastened on his. His arms automatically wrapped round her as she began the frenzied unfastening of his shirt and his belt buckle.

'Fiona . . .' he wrenched his mouth free.

'Mal . . .' Her hand slid inside his pants and she began to massage him.

'Fiona, I've something . . .'

'Not now, Mal. Mal, I've banked the fire up, we can do it on the rug again . . .'

Montgomerie's mortgaged two-bedroomed tenement in a sandstone terrace stood just off Queen Margaret Drive. Twenty minutes' walk away on the other side of Great Western Road stood a large house which had been broken up into a series of bedsitters. One of the rooms was rented by Detective-Sergeant Raymond Sussock. He lay in bed with WPC Willems beside him. They were sharing a cigarette.

'Don't mention it again,' she said, running her fingers over his chest.

'I can't get the cow out of my mind.'

'That's your problem. Just don't bring her into this bed.'

'She called me an old runt.'

'For God's sake, Ray.'

'She's got this technique of writing letters so that one phrase leaps out and hits you between the eyes.'

'I don't want to know.'

'It's annoying. I never thought it would be like this. I'm glad to be rid of her but at the same time I'll never be rid of her.'

'Ray, if you don't pack it in I'm leaving.'

'Sometimes I catch myself saying all the things I wanted to say to her but I'm only talking to the corner of the room.'

'You've flipped.'

'Maybe. Maybe it's just withdrawal symptoms.' He took

a deep breath.

'You're healthy enough, anyway,' she said as his chest sank. 'Nice strong beat from your ticker. Maybe you're not so old, Sussock.'

'You remember that time we were walking in the Winter Gardens and you told me to get out, clean break, with no half-measures?'

'Aye, that's when we were hunting the bampot with the knife. Fabian set me up and I'll never be able to wear a bikini again.'

Sussock hugged her. 'I owe you a lot for that bit of advice. My whole life's started again.'

'I also remember something else I said, something about no room for weak men in my life. I don't want to hear any more about it, otherwise I'll make a clean break of my own. OK?'

'OK.'

'C'mon, make love to me.'

'Again!'

'You can do it; c'mon, let me help you.'

It was Tuesday, 10 p.m.

King and Van der Veeght sat in Donoghue's office. Donoghue sat behind his desk, leaning back on his chair and pulling on his pipe. A silver coffee-pot stood on Donoghue's desk. It was 10.10 a.m. Wednesday.

'So, is that all?' said Van der Veeght, resting his notebook on his knee and reaching forward to take his cup from the Inspector's desk.

'It should be enough to go on,' replied Donoghue. 'We have a one-armed Dutchman called Frans Bakhuis who married a Scotswoman some years ago and fathered a girl three years ago. What we have to find out is when and why Domino Pahl returned to Scotland.'

King sat silently and stirred his coffee. His feedback had been well received and he did not want to over-intrude into the discussion.

'And we know that the mysterious lady in furs keeps her room in a mess and holds a Dutch passport in the name of Louisa Maartens,' Donoghue said, more to himself than to the others.

'I will wire that information to the Netherlands together with Detective-Constable King's information. I'm sure it will lead us somewhere.'

'Do that. When will you get a reply?'

'If I send it now, then I guess after lunch,' replied Van der Veeght.

Donoghue consulted his diary, laying well-manicured hands across the pages. 'Come and see me at three, please,' he said. 'I'm seeing a Sheriff in Chambers at four-thirty to apply for a warrant to search McFarlane's flat. I think I've already got grounds but every bit of information helps.'

'Very well.'

Van der Veeght and King stood. Donoghue asked King to remain behind and Van der Veeght left the room. Donoghue was impressed by Van der Veeght's lightness of step and silence of movement for one so big.

'WPC Willems will be joining us shortly, as will Montgomerie,' said Donoghue, pressing the charred tobacco into his pipe-bowl before flicking his old lighter. 'We have some work to allocate. You'd think a murder and a heroin haul would be sufficient, but . . .' he waved an upturned palm.

'Wishful thinking, sir,' said King.

'Maybe, but I expect pressure is why we both chose to work in Glasgow. There are always softer options open. What do you think of him?'

'Who?'

'Inspector Van der Veeght. What are your impressions?'

'Well . . .' King shifted uncomfortably. He knew he

held Donoghue's favour, he knew Donoghue had recommended him for promotion following the McPherson case, but there were times when such favour, far from being something to feel smug about, caused downright discomfort. King felt that this was such an occasion. This wasn't a friendly chat, they were both playing roles; Donoghue was in command — he even sat in a higher chair — and had done King the honour of soliciting his professional opinion. King knew he had to respond with an observation and not a non-committal answer. 'Well,' he said again.

Donoghue sat back and pulled on his pipe. The smoke was strong and sweet-smelling and hung in layers in the still air of his office. Behind him the window looked on to central Glasgow, the office blocks, the river, the expressways, the bars, the alleys, the gutters.

'He seems to be keen enough,' replied King at last. 'He was sensible enough to pull out of the hotel room when he didn't feel on top of the situation, and he didn't leave empty-handed.'

There was a reverential tap on Donoghue's door.

'Inspector Van der Veeght is a professional, King. You would do well to watch him work. Come in.'

Elka Willems entered the room, followed by Montgomerie, and Donoghue motioned them to sit down. WPC Willems, still managing to look elegant in functional uniform, sat in the chair recently vacated by Van der Veeght. Montgomerie, neat, slim and muscular, lifted a chair from against the wall and set it down next to King.

'A real professional,' said Donoghue to King. Elka Willems and Montgomerie glanced at each other. 'We have some work,' said Donoghue, taking two manilla folders from his drawer and laying them on his desk top. 'Chief Super Findlater wants us to allocate both. I'm in agreement with us acting on one but not the other, not yet anyway, not while we have the Pahl case on our hands.' He opened the first file. 'The most important one first. Sex attack in Kelvin Park. Not actual rape but a damn good try, lassie had enough sense to kick him hard where it hurts most and ran off. When our patrol arrived there was nobody in the park or round the gallery. This is yours, King, and I want you to work on it with WPC Willems.' Donoghue tossed the folder on to the edge of his desk and King reached forward and grasped it. 'The other, well . . .' Donoghue opened the second file and revealed two loose pieces of paper. Montgomerie recognized the first as the standard front sheet, a form giving name, address, date of birth, offence, date of inquiry/committal. He could see that the only part of the form that was filled in was the date of inquiry. The second piece of paper was a sheet of inexpensive stationery on which was some writing in a clumsy, large hand. There was a small brown envelope clipped to the sheet of stationery paper. Montgomerie didn't need to be told what it was.

'Anonymous letter,' said Donoghue. 'Alleging local government fraud. There might be nothing in it, but it might be the tip of the iceberg. You won't know until you've checked it out, Montgomerie.' He slid the file across the desk and Montgomerie reached for it. 'Let me know how you proceed with it, it's only being acted on because the boss wants it that way: it hasn't to take priority over the Pahl case.'

'I understand,' said Montgomerie.

'I'd like you to make some preliminary enquiries and come and see me this afternoon, say at four. We'll see what it looks like.'

'I get off at two, sir.'

Donoghue raised his eyebrows and relit his pipe.

'How old are you, Hazel?' asked Elka Willems.

'Nineteen.'

'Good. So we both know what we are talking about.'

Hazel Hanson glanced nervously towards the door. Her parents had volunteered to leave the room when Elka Willems explained the purpose of her visit and Hazel now fancied that they were standing in the hall with their ears pressed to the door.

'Don't worry about them,' said Elka Willems firmly. 'They won't hear anything. If you want to we can go to the station.'

'No.' Hazel Hanson sat back on the settee and curled her hand round the neck of the family's springer spaniel. She was a large girl, wide-eyed. Elka Willems thought the girl wouldn't have any difficulty with simple arithmetic, but she could forget being the next Brain of Britain. She seemed more bemused than upset by the incident.

Elka Willems felt that this was going to be a difficult interview. She sat back in the armchair and glanced around the room. The Hansons lived three-up in a three-roomed sandstone flat in Partick. The close was dripping with rainwater in half a dozen places, but the Hansons' flat seemed dry enough. It was a bit musty for Elka Willems's taste, and she felt it could do with a good clean-out, but the family wouldn't be catching pneumonia this winter. There was a brass coal-scuttle and shovel next to the hearth, and an old copy of the *Daily Record* stuck out from under the cushion of the other armchair as though it had been hastily pushed there when WPC Willems pressed the front doorbell. There was a battered wicker basket with wool and knitting-needles sticking out of the top, and a picture of the Queen on the wall.

'So you were walking down through Kelvin Park?'

Hazel Hanson nodded and began to wind the spaniel's ears round her fingers.

'What time?'

The girl shrugged her shoulders.

'What time?'

'Ten, ten-thirty.'

'Listen, Hazel, come on, sit up and listen. Leave the dog alone.' Elka Willems laid her ballpoint and her notebook on her lap and looked at the girl, who began to shift uncomfortably on the settee. 'Last night you were attacked and very nearly raped by a man who is obviously very dangerous and has to be caught before he can do this again. Now, we don't have all the time in the world, so please answer my questions as accurately as possible. Do you think you can do that?'

Hazel Hanson nodded, and Elka Willems saw the first faint trace of tears in the girl's eyes. Under her breath she said 'Heaven's sake' and picked up her ballpoint.

'So it was between ten and ten-thirty.'

The girl nodded.

'What were you doing out?'

'Walking.'

'Alone?'

A slight nod of the head. The shameful, guilty, awful admission of being nineteen, female, and having no one to walk with between 10 and 10.30 in the evening.

'Had you been drinking?'

A similar slight shake of the head that goes with the crushing sense of failure in not having a social life like in the magazines.

'You were just out walking?'

'Yes,' she said in a shaking voice. 'I haven't worked for a year. I'm in all day and it gets me down. Sometimes I just have to get out.'

'So what happened?'

'I was walking back. I'd gone to the top of the park and I was walking back.' She paused.

'Yes?'

'Well, he jumped out of the bushes at the side of me and grabbed me. He put one hand here.' She touched her breasts. 'And the other over my mouth, so I bit it.'

'Good girl.'

'He let go and I turned and kicked him. I read you have to do that. Then I ran off.'

'What did he look like?'

'I don't know.'

'You said you turned.'

'I did.'

'So what did he look like?'

'I don't know. He was wearing a mask.'

'What sort of mask?'

'A mask. Just a mask.'

'Hazel, there are lots of different types of mask. There are masks which just cover the eyes and masks which cover the face, there are paper masks and plastic masks and expensive rubber masks. There are masks which look like human faces and masks which look like Dracula and masks which look like gorillas. So what kind of mask was he wearing?'

'Oh,' said Hazel Hanson.

'Well!'

'None of these,' she said.

'Hazel, you're not making things easy for me.' Hazel Hanson was in fact making things very difficult for a hard-pressed WPC. Elka Willems found herself wanting to be short with the girl, but checked herself, taking a deep breath instead. 'Can you tell me what the mask looked like, then?'

'Yes. It was a clown's mask.'

'A clown's face?'

'Sort of pink with big red lips and a mouth that was laughing. But that didn't fit with the sound.'

'What sound?'

'The sound he made when I bit him.'

'God preserve us,' sighed Elka Willems, and then, in a

tone of forced enthusiasm, said: 'Right, now we're getting somewhere.'

'We are?' asked Hazel Hanson.

'Yes. We know he was wearing a mask which looked like a clown's face.'

'Is that important?' Hazel Hanson smiled.

'Well, Hazel, it could be. Now let's see if we can find out anything else about him. The hand he put over your mouth, was it his right or his left hand?'

The girl sat forward and made slow and clumsy motions of putting her hand over the mouth of a person whom she imagined standing with his back towards her. She did it first with her left hand and then, after some deliberation, with her right. She sat back and held up an arm. 'This one,' she said.

'His left?'

'I think so.'

'So he may be a left-hander.' Elka Willems scribbled in her notebook. 'Now his size. Was he big or small?'

'Sort of average.'

'I thought you'd say that, somehow. Was he as tall as me, or taller, or shorter?'

'Bit smaller.'

Elka Willems thought he was probably a lot smaller. She knew Ray Sussock admired her for many reasons, not the least of which was her looks. He had more than once called her a 'Nordic Goddess', not only because of her striking features, but also because she stood five feet ten inches tall and still managed to weigh less than ten stone.

'How much smaller?'

'A bit.'

A clock on the wall chimed midday.

'Well, was he taller than you?'

'A bit.'

'I see. Was he a bit more taller than you than he was a bit smaller than me?'

'Oh, a bit more taller than me.'

Elka Willems felt she had cracked a speech code. In her notebook she wrote, '5' 5"/7"?'

'Was he thin or fat?'

'Sort of round.'

'Chubby?'

'No, just round.'

'Long legs?'

'No, not especially long. Not as long as yours, if you don't mind me saying, miss.'

'Not at all. What was he wearing?'

'Jeans and a jacket.'

'What sort of jacket, denim, leather?'

'No. A jacket like soldiers wear.'

'A combat jacket?'

'Is that what they're called?'

'Sort of splodgy different shades of green, comes down to here.' She tapped her thigh.

'Yes.'

'That's a combat jacket.'

'Oh.'

'Age, now. Was he young or old?'

'Not young, not old.'

'Was he older than you, Hazel?'

'I don't know. I didn't see his face.'

'Well, did he move like a young man or was he slow?'

'He was quite fast.'

'Strong?'

'Not as strong as my dad.'

'Your dad's strong, is he?'

'He used to be a wrestler till his back went.'

'I think we can say he's a young man. He seemed to scarper quickly enough. We got to the park two mintues after your call. How long between the attack and your call, Hazel?'

'Five, ten minutes. I don't really know.'

'OK. Now, did he have any sort of smell?'

'Like what?'

'Well, did he smell dirty like a tramp, did he smell of alcohol?'

'No.'

'No smell?'

'No, he didn't smell like that.'

'Heaven's sake! How did he smell?'

'Sort of nice.'

'Nice!'

'Like perfume.'

'You mean aftershave?'

'Is that what it's called?'

Elka Willems scribbled.

'Is that important?' asked Hazel Hanson.

'Maybe. It may indicate he's clean-shaven. It certainly means he's not a dosser or a heavy drinker. Probably a very clean-living person.'

Hazel Hanson smiled.

'So we have a left-handed male, say about five feet seven, not heavily built but no scarecrow either, denims, combat jacket, probably clean-shaven, probably fixed abode. Age? Twenties, early thirties. Anything else you'd like to tell me?'

'No, not really, 'cept one thing. When he pulled me towards him, I felt something in my back.'

'A knife?'

'No, these.' She touched her breasts for the second time. 'But it couldn't have been, could it? Only men attack girls. Don't they?'

Inside, Elka Willems began a long, loud scream.

Montgomerie drained his mug of coffee and read the note over again. It was written in black ballpoint and badly smudged. The paper was small and heavily lined, as though from a childs stationery set. It read:

Sir,

Councillor Floyd is so bent he looks straight. He took a back-hander from Torvaney-Stuart for the road-widening job last September. He's at it again, the bastard, you can see them together in the Bells of Hell, Thursdays p.m.

Sorry no name.

The envelope was a small brown one with a second-class stamp stuck nearer the centre than the top right-hand corner. It was addressed to 'The Police, Charing Cross, Glasgow', had been posted on the first of the month, and, according to the mailroom stamp had been received that morning, Wednesday the third.

Montgomerie filled out the front sheet of the file.

Name   Floyd, Gavin, Cllr.

Address   39 Glamis Causeway, Easterhouse.

Complaint   Alleged Corrupt Practices.

Source of Complaint   Letter (anonymous).

Division   P, Charing Cross, Glasgow, G 3.

Officer in Charge   DC Montgomerie.

3/11 Acting on information received am to investigate activities of Cllr. Floyd in respect of alleged corruption. Investigation to be clandestine in first instance.

He closed the file and slipped it, spine up, into his grey metal filing cabinet. He went to the central office and consulted a wall chart entitled 'Know your Regional Councillor', locating Councillor Floyd among the battery of inch-square mug shots. Floyd was a bald-headed man in his fifties who wore thick-framed spectacles and was smiling benignly at the camera. There was a small biography underneath each photograph, Floyd's history being that he had served on the Regional Council for fifteen years as an Independent, the last three of which had seen him the chairman of the Roads and Highways committee, which was a sub-committee of the Building and General Works committee. It was 12.10 p.m.

Montgomerie hustled himself a quick snack of beans on toast in what was optimistically referred to as 'the canteen'. It never failed to amaze him how a room with only chairs and four tables and one three-ringed cooker could provide victualling facilities for a staff complement of 97. It seemed to operate with an unofficial sittings system, with most people accepting the need to get in and get out, especially at weekday lunchtimes when the day shift had to share with the clerical back-up team. Montgomerie finished his meal and rinsed his plate in the sink. Then he drove across the town to George Square and the City Chambers, where he asked a bemused official for minutes of the meetings of the sub-committee on Roads and Highways. He took the ledger to a table and began to turn the pages.

On September 12th last year under the chairmanship of Councillor Floyd, the committee had approved a tender from Torvaney-Stuart quoting £150,000 to widen a three-mile stretch of arterial road in the south side. Montgomerie checked back over the weekly meetings of the committee for a further twelve months and then checked forward to the minutes of the last meeting. At the end of two hours Montgomerie's eyes were sore and his back was beginning to go. In his notebook he had recorded:

current *financial year*	1st Aug—	Approved Torvaney-Stuart tender value			£120,000
	15th May—	"	"	"	£135,000
previous *financial year*	3rd Jan—	"	"	"	£200,000
	12th Sep—	"	"	"	£150,000

second previous *financial year*	20th Dec—	Approved Torvaney- Stuart tender value	£157,000
	11th Jul—	" " "	£175,000
		total value over previous 31 months	£937,000

It had taken Montgomerie two hours to gnaw that information from the minutes and he was beginning to feel under time pressure. He didn't have another two hours to go back to when Floyd assumed chairmanship of the committee, but he felt he had enough to be working on. All the contracts were for small-scale operations; road-widening, earth-moving, foundation-laying; there was nothing like the £45-million contracts given to the big companies to build motorways through the centre of the city and over the river to link up with the motorway on the other side, and when looked at in the context of 31 months of Regional Council spending, the £937,000 looked like change from a good night out. But even so, if Floyd was getting a straight 2% rake-off then he was on Easy Street. Montgomerie took the hypothetical 2%, scribbled on his pad and came up with the figure of £18,000 plus, all for Floyd's pocket. But it was a big 'if' and there was nothing conclusive, and Montgomerie reminded himself that nine out of ten anonymous letters prove to be smoke without any fire. Torvaney-Stuart might be an up-and-coming Quaker firm run by good men and true, and Councillor Floyd might be so straight he looked bent. Montgomerie asked the official for the file containing details of tenders submitted to the Roads and Highways sub-committee. He was given a box-file containing photocopies and he selected the tenders discussed at the meeting of the committee on 1st August. There were three tenders submitted for a contract to lay a new exit road from a congested industrial estate.

Torvaney-Stuart had submitted a tender for £120,000.

J W McKenzie & Co Ltd had submitted a tender for £110,000.

Pavase (UK) Holdings Ltd had submitted a tender for £95,000.

Montgomerie read over the minutes of the meeting of the committee on the 1st August.

Item		Action
9	Tenders for road construction at Craigievar Industrial Estate to provide second exit to Leith Rd.	
	The committee considered the three tenders submitted by the closing time. The chairman reminded the committee of the previous high standard of work done by Torvaney-Stuart and expressed his opinion that their tender should be accepted despite the sum proposed.	
	There was majority agreement.	to Executive for approval
	Cllrs Young and McDonald wished their disagreement to be minuted.	

The letterhead of the Torvaney-Stuart tender gave the company's managing director as one Chas. Stuart, and the company's head office as 'Benbecula', the Esplanade, Helensburgh.

It was 2.30 p.m. and Montgomerie snapped the box-file shut and handed it and the ledger back to the official. He was conscious of the short time before his meeting with Donoghue at four to discuss the allegation. He drove back to the police station, phoned down to the computer terminal requesting information on Charles Stuart of 'Benbecula', Helensburgh, signed a 135mm SLR with telephoto lens out of stores and drove out to Easterhouse, parking the car three hundred yards from the Floyds' close on Glamis Causeway.

It was a long shot which paid off. Easterhouse wasn't Montgomerie's favourite place in Big G. Its few small shops had metal plates for windows, so strangers and newcomers had to go inside before they knew what the shop sold. Montgomerie could have sat in his car for an hour surrounded by jerry-built houses and listless unemployed youth in the gathering November gloom before driving back to the station with nothing to show for his vigil. At 3.35 he had given himself five more minutes before the drive back. At 3.37 Councillor and Mrs Floyd stepped out of the close mouth of 39 Glamis Causeway and walked towards a car. Montgomerie shot ten frames and then looked at the Floyds more closely through the telephoto lens. He was reminded of Donoghue's anecdote of catching a bent councillor because his wife went to the supermarket in her curlers and mink coat. Mrs Floyd wasn't any fur-wrapped floozie in a two-thousand-quid mink, but she wasn't wearing a WRVS handout, either. The car they got into was a Volvo estate. It was a few years old but it was still a Volvo, which, Montgomerie thought, was pretty good going for G 34.

He returned to Charing Cross and gave the spool to Jimmy Bothwell to develop. He checked his pigeonhole. There was the Police National Computer print-out on Charles Stuart. Stuart was fifty-three years old. Two years previously he had been fined £1,000 for fraud and ten years previously had done eighteen months of a two-year sentence in Saughton for embezzlement. His file was held by the Grampian Police following his involvement in a brawl in Dundee twelve months previously. Montgomerie wrote up his case notes, putting himself into it, considering angles, and gave his professional opinion that there was something nasty in the woodshed. It was 4.05 p.m. He walked along the corridor to Donoghue's office.

CHAPTER 6

Wednesday: 5 p.m.

It couldn't have been called a conference, and was hastily minuted as a review meeting between Donoghue, Van der Veeght, King, Sussock, and Chief Superintendent Findlater, who had accepted Donoghue's short-notice invitation to attend. Donoghue gave up his chair to Findlater and sat with the others in front of his desk. Elka Willems sat at the side of the room with a notebook on her lap, scribbling in shorthand.

'So it is all a mystery,' said Van der Veeght, leafing through a photocopy of the Telex message from the Royal Netherlands Police. They all had a copy, except WPC Willems. Findlater clasped the original in his huge hands.

'Not at all,' replied Donoghue, taking his pipe from his mouth.

'It doesn't tell us who she is.'

'It tells us who she isn't,' said Donoghue. 'She is not Louisa Maartens, aged thirty-two, private secretary. According to this report Louisa Maartens died two weeks ago, found in her apartment in Amsterdam, with 280 milligrams of pure heroin in her veins. You can knock out a herd of elephants with that amount. She must have been blown apart.'

'Yes. But it is still a mystery.' The burly Dutchman leaned forward and rested his right hand on his right knee. 'Louisa Maartens dies in Amsterdam and shortly afterwards a woman assumes her identity and arrives in Glasgow a few hours before Dominique Pahl is also murdered in a similar way.'

'There's an obvious connection,' said Donoghue. 'I think the woman in fur is connected with both murders.'

'I agree,' said Van der Veeght. 'You and I, Inspector, obviously have a different notion of what is a mystery. For you something stops being a mystery when you begin to know something. For me it is a mystery until I know everything.'

'Perhaps you are right,' said Donoghue drily. He put his pipe back in his mouth and pulled on it.

'Shall we get on?' grunted Findlater.

'So.' Van der Veeght held a finger in the air. 'So. Dominique Pahl's husband, Frans Bakhuis with one arm, died eighteen months ago. He was found near the Ijsselmeer with a burst-open stomach. In Holland we have cross-indexed our files. Now, there was once an arrest and the man arrested gave information in return for leniency. I think you have a phrase, "turned evidence" . . .?'

'Turned Queen's evidence,' said Donoghue.

'So. Now, gentlemen, you will see from the sheets the third page is in Dutch and so is the fourth; you might say it is double-dutch.'

Donoghue and King responded with an obligatory chuckle. Findlater's expression remained as warm as an iceberg.

'Now I will translate.' Van der Veeght studied the sheet for a moment and then began to read haltingly. 'I, Joseph de Vries, am making this statement of my own free will and I am not under intimidation or duress. I understand that this statement will not guarantee leniency of the court.

'I am telling you of the time they killed the one-armed man. I have seen death before, in Algeria, I am not a stranger to it, but this is horrible.

'I do not know the full story. We were brought to

watch. I think none of us knew the full story, but later, when I had been with the organization some years and I talked with another courier, I found out about the one-armed man.

'He was also a courier, bringing horse from the east to Europe, to Amsterdam. The one-armed man never harmed the organization but he tried to leave it. With his wife and child he went someplace but he couldn't escape which is why you must protect me. They found him and brought him back.

'They took us to a warehouse and he was tied to the floor so he couldn't move and his wife was there, a pretty girl and she was screaming. All the time she was screaming. They forced water into his mouth until it came through his stomach. Many men fainted. Then they say to the woman now you will work for us, we have your child so you must work for us.'

'God's sake!' hissed Donoghue.

'The man who killed the one-armed man was not Chinese. He was one in the organization who was part of the police force . . .'

'Police force!' Findlater gasped.

'I think, sir,' Van der Veeght moved his arm in a circular motion as he grasped for words, 'he means a police force within the organization.'

'Thugs and bully boys to keep the rest in line,' said Donoghue.

'Thank you,' said Van der Veeght. 'That is what he means. So, he then says: I have not seen them since. This is all I know of the one-armed man.'

Van der Veeght folded his photocopy of the report and looked at the floor, waiting for somebody to say something. For a while there was a heavy silence, broken when Donoghue struck a match, lit his pipe, and asked if the Royal Netherlands Police knew where the child was.

'No,' said Van der Veeght. 'We need more information

about the child and the organization.'

'I'd say it was a big area of concern for you. After all, it is a kidnapping.'

'Please do not tell us our job,' said Van der Veeght coldly. 'I'm sure it is being acted upon following this fellow making the statement.'

'It was made months ago,' said Donoghue, looking at the top of his copy. 'I take it "Mei" is Dutch for May.'

'Gentlemen!' Findlater reared forward. 'We can leave it to the Dutch police to trace the child, and we will give them every assistance.'

'Thank you,' said Van der Veeght, staring coldly at Donoghue.

'It's a very upsetting statement,' King said, sensing the sudden tension between Donoghue and Van der Veeght. 'We know now why she didn't put up any resistance when she heard the dead knock, I mean if the alternative was running and suffering the same fate as her husband. She also seems to have less faith in protective custody than the man who made this statement.'

'Unless she felt the organization, the Triad, would kill her child if it did not kill her,' said Van der Veeght softly.

'Dear God,' said King, who had a child aged three, his youngest.

'Well,' began Donoghue, 'we have a motive for Dominique Pahl's death; she messed up a consignment, and she could neither run nor inform the police because the Triad has her child. We have a mysterious woman in furs who arrived in Glasgow just prior to the Pahl woman's death, and who is taken out by a young man with expensive tastes who just happens to be a van-boy with the company which imported heroin with its prawns. What do you think?'

'I think it stinks,' said Findlater.

'We need to turn over the woman's room,' said King. 'We need to find out who she is.'

'I agree,' said Donoghue. 'I also think we ought to turn over McFarlane's flat. We'll do both this evening, I think, Chief Superintendent.'

'I think you ought,' said Findlater. 'Who will do what?'

'Well, I suggest King has a look at the woman's hotel room and Heer Van der Veeght, along with Montgomerie, visits McFarlane's flat.'

'Very well,' said Findlater.

'Montgomerie?' asked Van der Veeght. 'He was . . . ?'

'The officer who met you at the airport,' said Donoghue.

Van der Veeght grunted his thanks.

'Any areas not covered?' Findlater began to fold his copy of the report.

'Inspector,' said Van der Veeght turning to Donoghue. 'You said that you found a recent photograph of the child in Dominique Pahl's house?'

'Yes. And a notebook with coded entries. Montgomerie is giving his full attention to the latter.'

'The child, I think I read in the report, seemed to be about three when the photograph was taken.'

'Uh-huh.' Donoghue pulled on his pipe.

'So,' the Dutchman sat forward a little, 'If Heer Bakhuis was murdered eighteen months ago and the child kidnapped at the same time, then the child must have been about eighteen months old when she was snatched.'

'My God,' said Donoghue. 'I see what you mean.'

'I don't,' said Findlater.

'With each delivery there must have been a photograph of the child,' said Van der Veeght. 'To show she was still alive and well and to keep Dominique Pahl in the organization. Inspector Donoghue, you asked me once if I could think of a reason to go to her house then you would agree to me going there. I now have a reason; I think there must be eighteen more photographs of the child hidden in the house.'

'By all means,' said Donoghue, feeling uncomfortable for not seeing the possibility himself.

'They may help to trace her, especially if they are outside shots; they may locate her.'

'By all means,' said Donoghue again. 'When would you like to go?'

'This afternoon, now, straight after the meeting.' Van der Veeght looked at his watch. 'It's five-forty-five—we should be back by seven-thirty, in time to visit the flat of Mr McFarlane.'

'Good. Will you take Montgomerie with you if he's still in the building?'

Elka Willems closed her notebook. Like King, she had sensed the tension between Donoghue and Van der Veeght, and she also thought that Donoghue had to concede a point to the Dutchman. She thought it must not have been easy for him to argue his case in a foreign police department in a foreign language. It wasn't just that Van der Veeght was a handsome Dutchman like her father that made Elka Willems follow him with her eyes as he left Donoghue's office.

Van der Veeght and Montgomerie let themselves into 188 Matilda Avenue with the key which had been found among Dominique Pahl's personal effects. The house was in semi-darkness, with the last rays of daylight streaming through the south-facing windows. It was very quiet and very still; it was chilly and was beginning to develop a musty smell.

'Do you think there will be a ghost?' asked Van der Veeght.

'Bullshit.' Montgomerie reached up to the lever just inside the front door and switched the mains supply on. Then he flicked the hall light on.

'It's not bullshit. I saw a ghost once. It was a strange

experience, but even stranger was that I felt no fear. No fear at all.'

'Tell me about it some time,' said Montgomerie.

'I will. Where do you think she hid the photographs?'

'Haven't a clue. Why do you think she had to hide them? I mean, if they were given to her by this Triad organization to keep her sweet as you say they were, why hide them from the very people who gave them to her?'

'That's what the inspector said,' replied Van der Veeght. 'After the conference when we were walking in the corridor. You weren't there.'

'I wasn't invited,' replied Montgomerie, drily.

'I don't know the answer,' said Van der Veeght.

The two men walked down the hall to the front room. Montgomerie switched on the light over the chesterfields, the oak panelling, the books lining the wall.

'She was found here,' said Montgomerie. 'Sitting in this chair.'

'Such a dull room to die in.' Van der Veeght's eyes swept around the room. Large, expensively decorated and furnished; cold; deadly. 'It is not a happy room.'

'Sort of Modern Homes Exhibition 1920,' said Montgomerie.

'Sorry?'

'I mean it's kind of old-style decoration.'

'Yes. It's very sad, this room.'

'It's a sad house.' Montgomerie pushed his hands deep into his jacket pocket and shivered. 'No, what we were saying bothers me.'

'Hiding the photographs?'

'Aye, I can't see the point.'

'We may find the answer to that when we find the photographs,' said Van der Veeght. 'Or when you crack the coded notebook. Are you making progress, Malcolm?'

'I'm working on it,' said Montgomerie.

'It will be crucial.'

'How do you know?'

'Believe me, I know.'

'OK, we'll see, I dare say. I suggest we start with her bedroom. That's where they found the notebook, stuffed among her knickers.'

The photographs were not in Dominique Pahl's bedroom. They were not in any of the drawers, they were not under the mattress, they were not under the carpet, nor slipped behind the wallpaper, nor folded and pushed inside the hollow lampstand, nor were they pressed inside the picture-frames behind the paintings. After forty-five minutes they were satisfied that Dominique Pahl's bedroom was 'clean'.

The photographs were not in the drawing-room. They were not trapped between the old books, or stuck underneath the coffee-table or pushed up the chimney-back.

Neither were they in the junk-room which seemed to be used for storing odd bits of furniture. The lock was forced on a promising-looking briefcase which in the event turned out to contain sheet music and invoices from Laing & Co. dated June 1902. They were brown, and crumpled at a touch. They found a loose floorboard in an empty room, under which was nothing but cobwebs. Montgomerie emerged from the cellar holding his flashlight in one hand and dusting himself off with the other. He looked at Van der Veeght and shook his head.

6.45. Montgomerie and Van der Veeght sat in the drawing-room. Montgomerie sprawled out on the settee, not caring about the dust he was grinding into the polished hide. Van der Veeght sat statesmanlike in the chair in which Dominique Pahl had been found.

'We'll be doing this again in less than an hour,' said Van der Veeght.

'A bit more delicately, I hope,' replied Montgomerie. 'But you're right, we're running short of time.'

'So, Malcolm, you are hiding something from someone, where would you hide it?'

'Dunno. Best place to hide a tree is in a forest. In this case I reckon I'd outsmart them. Put it right under their noses.'

'So, I think, would I.'

They found the photographs in the guest-room, in an unsealed manilla envelope underneath the mattress of the single bed. There were ten photographs in all, not the eighteen they had expected, but none the less they were of the same child, and it seemed, showed her growing quite happily. According to the dates pencilled on the back, the photographs spanned a period of twenty months. The photographs were in black-and-white and measured approximately 6 inches by 10. The first four showed the child in a crib, the later six showed her outside a small house, and the background seemed to be aspects of the same village. The second last photograph also showed a road sign, just above the child's head; it was in the distance, but even without the aid of a magnifying glass both men could clearly read 'Aunspeet — 4 km'.

'That was careless,' said Van der Veeght. 'With these, particularly this one, we can locate her. I only hope that we are in time.'

'What do you mean?'

'Well, now Dominique Pahl is dead what use do they have for her child?'

'My God,' croaked Montgomerie. He felt weak at the knees.

'I will wire all those photographs to Holland when we get back to the station, Malcolm. I will insist on doing so before we go out to visit McFarlane's flat.'

'I don't think you'll meet any objection,' said Montgomerie.

Also in the envelope they found a dozen small sheets of writing-paper on which a series of numbers had been written in a hurried but painstaking hand.

'Something else for you to work on, Malcolm.'

'Does it ever stop?' said Montgomerie.

'Let us press on, Malcolm.' Van der Veeght put the photographs and the sheets of paper back into the envelope and hurried out of the house, carrying Montgomerie in his wake.

At 7.30 p.m. Montgomerie and Van der Veeght were on observation outside McFarlane's flat in Partick. King and Sussock were on observation outside the Antonine. Donoghue sat by the radio control console in the basement of P Division. Outside he could hear the rumble of the motorway traffic as it thundered under Charing Cross. He knew both teams would be under time pressure, especially Montgomerie and Van der Veeght, and he was worried about King, who was to be operating solo.

Montgomerie watched a pretty girl in western boots walk by the car, and then returned his gaze to the close mouth of 197. McFarlane appeared, well groomed in a velvet suit. He walked towards his low-slung and highly polished car. Montgomerie nudged Van der Veeght, who wiped his eyes and grunted. He reached for the microphone which hung under the dashboard of their car.

'Unit One. He's on his way. We'll give him five minutes before we move. Over.'

Montgomerie released the switch on the mouthpiece and heard the crackly voice of a woman police constable say 'Acknowledged'.

In the control-room Donoghue leaned forward, reached over the shoulder of the WPC and pressed the 'send' button at the base of the large microphone. He called up King and Sussock, Unit Two, and advised them of McFarlane's departure. He released the button, stood back, reaching for his pipe, and heard Sussock's gravelly voice through the static, 'Roger'.

It was 7.35 p.m.

Montgomerie glanced at his watch and got out of the car. Van der Veeght slid across and took Montgomerie's place in the driving seat.

'Three blasts on the horn means he's on his way back,' said the Dutchman. 'Four means he's back and you have a problem, Malcolm.'

'Thanks a bunch,' said Montgomerie. He pulled his collar up against the wind and walked across the street to McFarlane's close.

It was a clean and well-lit stair, a self-respecting close. It was the sort of stair where the residents don't hesitate to reach for the phone and dial the number on the poster headed 'Complaints about stair lighting' which was pasted high on the wall near the entrance of the close. The stair was swept and brushed and had a strong scent of disinfectant. McFarlane lived in one of the two top flats. His door was heavy and painted with black gloss paint. The door handle and letterbox were made of brass and McFarlane's nameplate was one of white letters embossed on an elaborate background. Montgomerie stood in front of the door and played safe by rapping the knocker, which was hinged on the letterbox. The hammering echoed down the four stone flights of stair. There was no response from anywhere on the stair, or, more importantly, from behind the door. McFarlane lived alone and he didn't keep a dog. Like most people in Glasgow McFarlane had more than one lock on his door, but he was unlike them in the number he chose. While most folk settled for two, McFarlane had four. Montgomerie hissed 'damn!' and then checked the locks closely. He took a bunch of keys from his pocket and, working from top to bottom, had unlocked the three mortise locks within two minutes. The fourth, a barrel lock, yielded to gentle pressure from his shoulder and the delicate handling of a credit card.

McFarlane's flat was all wrong. Montgomerie didn't know what to expect — the doss of a struggling van-lad, or a lavish six-roomed pad belonging to suave McFarlane, man about town, or else something between the two. But this was something else.

The first thing that hit Montgomerie was the smell, not quite a stench but just short of being strong enough to make the air chewable. The smell was unmistakable to anyone who had spent hours in dim rooms listening to weird music while engaging in half-explored relationships, or had strolled across the grass at rock festivals in Indian Moccasins, but there was something more than being laid back in burning incense like that. Montgomerie shut the door behind him and listened. The flat was silent, save for the soft jingling of bells which had been stirred by the opening and the closing of the door. Montgomerie felt for the light-switch, shut his eyes and flicked the hall light on.

The visual impact was as striking as the smell. It was a sombre, dark-painted flat; a colour scheme consisting of purple and black but with odd streaks of gold here and there. Beads instead of doors hung at the entrance of each room. Odd oriental images hung on the wall and a series of small Buddhas stood in a line along the hallway floor. In the largest room two chaises stood facing each other, draped in black shawls. They stood on a brown rug. There was a bedroom with a big brass bed with black sheets and dark blankets. The remains of a long joss-stick smouldered in the grate. There was a walk-in wardrobe with slatted vents, a nice piece of furniture, but spoilt, to Montgomerie's taste, by being painted black. He tried the metal catch but it was locked. He poked at it with the thin metal spike on his penknife, but it wouldn't give. He was disappointed; wardrobes say a great deal about a person, they are second only to the kitchen in the information they contain.

McFarlane seemed to do a great deal of his living in the kitchen, and it was in the kitchen that Montgomerie knew he would find one of the things that he was looking for: an odd article which would be carrying McFarlane's fingerprints and which could be removed without McFarlane noticing its absence. Montgomerie found it in the waste-bin. Poking deep inside the bin-liner he came across a tin which looked as though it had once contained fruit and which had been stripped of its label. Montgomerie gripped the rim of the can between thumb and forefinger and dropped it into one of the self-sealing cellophane packages he carried. He left the sachet on top of the old refrigerator and walked around the kitchen.

There wasn't a deal to walk around. It was a twelve-by-ten room with an old sink of galvanized iron which would be described by the property agents as 'serviceable', in which McFarlane had left at least two days' washing up. He seemed to live out of tins: a bean floated in the grey water. The floor was covered with old newspapers, the light-bulb was naked. In the corner lay an old pair of jeans, a Canadian-style jacket, and a pair of worn working-boots. Donald McFarlane's (van-lad) working clothes.

Donald McFarlane (man about town) parked his car neatly against the kerb outside the Antonine and walked into the hotel, tossing the car keys up and down in his hand. Ray Sussock reached forward and snatched the microphone from the dashboard.

'He's on his way in, chief,' he said. 'The smooth bastard.'

'Steady, Ray.' Donoghue stood in front of the radio console and held the microphone delicately at chest height as he would a half-pint of Guinness at a reception. 'He's just under suspicion, that's all.'

'He's as guilty as hell. Did you hear the things the

Dutchman was saying this afternoon? I still can't believe half of what I heard.'

'Just go easy, Ray.'

'He's getting to me.'

Donoghue didn't respond. He called Van der Veeght and advised him of McFarlane's imminent return. Donoghue replaced the microphone on the console desk and returned to the chair in the corner of the room, leaving the WPC in a crisp white shirt sniffing involuntarily at the cloud of aftershave scent and tobacco smoke which hung around her.

Inside McFarlane's flat Montgomerie heard three sharp blasts on a car's horn. He grabbed the polythene sachet off the refrigerator, switched off the lights, pulled the door shut behind him and locked the three mortise locks. In the car he tossed the sachet on to the back seat.

'You have found something, Malcolm?' Van der Veeght started the engine.

'Perhaps,' replied Montgomerie. 'Perhaps.'

Outside the Antonine Hotel Dick King slipped out of the passenger door of the unmarked Ford and melted into the night. Ray Sussock waited in the car, tapping his palms on the steering-wheel, until McFarlane re-appeared with his lady-friend, escorted her to his saloon and then started the car. King leaned into a shop doorway, and only when McFarlane drove his car smoothly and silently away, followed by Ray Sussock in the battered back-firing police department heap, did he throw his cigarette to the ground and walk towards the hotel. He smiled at the girl behind the reception desk and started up the stairs at a brisk pace, feeling the girl's curious stare burning into his back. He was continually amazed at what he could get away with if he used the 'brass neck' approach.

He walked to room 235, tapped on the door and strolled away down the corridor. He stood at the end of the corridor and waited. Nothing. No one. Silence. He walked back towards the door, taking his credit card from his wallet as he did so.

He'd been warned to expect a mess, but even so he was jolted by the state of the room. Louisa Maartens's room, or rather the room which had been booked by an as yet to be identified person in the name of Louisa Maartens, reminded King of middle-class homes following a break-in by thieves who not only want to steal but also want to wreck the place, spray paint on the walls and shit in the drawers. He too felt the sense of danger that had upset Van der Veeght two nights earlier, the same feeling that this mess was in some designed, ordered, created specially to entrap unwary police officers.

It stank. It froze him to the ground just inside the door. He felt something rotten in the room. Something evil, something bigger than anything he had experienced. He steeled himself against his impulse to run, and focused his thoughts. He knew he needed something which would identify the occupant of the room. It had to be something she would not miss, but the nature of his feelings, the state of the room, were such that he sensed danger in taking something from the waste-bin. Anyone who is remotely wary of police operations concerning themselves know that nothing is thrown away: if anything is to be discarded it has to be destroyed. For three or four minutes he stood silently, and then inched forward, over nylon tights, shoes with thin heels, chiffon scarves, and a necklace in danger of being consumed by the pile. He edged across the bedroom floor and into the bathroom. The bathroom was neater, the towels hung more or less where they ought to hang, and the bar of soap was resting at the side of the bath, only inches from the recess in the wall where it was supposed to rest. The bathroom would need some honest-to-God scrubbing before the next guest could move in, yet it was more relaxed, more human than the bedroom. King thought that if anything could be removed from room 235 without the occupant noticing it would have to be removed from the bathroom. He noticed two glass tumblers on a shelf above the wash-basin and he picked one up and dropped it into a self-sealing polythene sachet. He knew he had taken a gamble—a tumbler is a large object and may be missed immediately—but he knew they needed information, and needed it yesterday. Also on the bathroom shelf with the tumblers was a heavy safety razor, not the chic light-weight female version he would have expected. He didn't dwell on it; it didn't matter what tool was used, he thought, so long as the job was done. He retraced his steps across the bedroom floor and stepped into the corridor, experiencing the same unsettling experience as Van der Veeght of having narrowly escaped from something.

In the foyer he noticed the receptionist was absent. He walked over to the desk and spun the register towards him. He turned the pages back. Room 235 had been occupied by the present guest on October 31st, the day before Dominique Pahl was murdered.

Montgomerie's monthly payslip left him little to buy food and clothing once the building society had taken its cut. What he got in return was an old but substantial three-roomed flat in a sandstone terrace, in which to live with the wonderful feeling that nobody could give him notice to quit.

Fiona had let herself into Montgomerie's flat. She had cooked a meal and placed it in the oven to keep warm. She peeled off her work clothes and stepped into a hot bath, having softened the water with herb-scented cubes. She patted herself dry with Montgomerie's huge blue towel, slipped into a jet-black low-cut split-thigh dress, and waited for Montgomerie. It was 8 p.m.

At 9 p.m., two glasses of wine later, she was still

waiting. She knew Montgomerie was supposed to finish at
2 p.m. that day, she also knew he had to work overtime
on occasions, but, angrily, felt that working an extra
seven hours was edging on the ridiculous. She read the
Evening Times again and did the crossword. Still no
Malcolm; no tall, slim-hipped male loping into the
lounge, no arms holding her, no chest for her to run her
hands over. She moved across the room to turn on the
television, intent out of sheer anger on destroying the
mood she had created, when she saw the book. It was
lying on the floor where Montgomerie had flung it three
nights ago, dismissing his boss as a 'bloody smooth
Edinbrovian bloody slave-driver'. It was no ordinary
notebook—roughly A5 in dimension, a little thicker than
an exercise book, and bound richly in dark brown
patterned leather. She reached down and picked it up.

She flicked through the book. Most pages were blank
but some, she guessed just less than half, contained blocks
of numbers. Intrigued, she took some scrap paper and an
old ballpoint pen and sat with the book at the table. She
turned the pages of the book and stopped at one page,
not so much at random, but more because the pattern of
numbers pleased her:

```
132172151129924        5217176114215
1943        24184162518154        1617152416162
92221211        1277911
11217521592411116
```

It seemed to her that the numbers must represent
letters and so she drew up the alphabet and numbered the
letters, A being 1, B being 2. Then she applied her
formula and got nowhere. She reversed it, A being 26, B
being 25, and got no further. She moved each letter back
one so that A was 26, B was 1; nothing. She moved them
forward one; A was 2, B was 3; nothing. She put the pen

down and looked at the overall pattern of numbers. It seemed that 1 might represent S, the second most commonly used letter. She tried to apply that theory but could not, and so went back to her trial and error method. Only when she applied the theory that the letters had been numbered from D rather than A did she get somewhere. It was still by trial and error that she had to find out whether, for instance, 16 was DI, or S, or just numbers as they stood. Eventually she was left with:

Peternella Hettinger
1943 Augsburg Strasse
Leyden 127911
Netherlands

Following a habit she had picked up from Montgomerie, she made herself a mug of coffee and set to work.

CHAPTER 7

By 8.30 p.m. on Wednesday, 3rd November, three sets of fingerprints had been lifted in connection with the investigation, two from the tumbler taken from the bathroom at the Antonine Hotel, and a third set taken from the can which Montgomerie had dug from the depths of the waste-bin under McFarlane's sink unit. By 9 p.m. Jimmy Bothwell had processed the sets of prints and had started feeding the information into the Police National Computer, using the terminal in the basement of P Division. Copies of the three sets of prints were also telexed to the Royal Netherlands Police. By 9.15 all there was to do was wait. Montgomerie and King signed off duty, went to a bar with Van der Veeght, and then melted separately into the night. Donoghue, tiring of cars for the second time that week, returned home to Edinburgh by train. Ray Sussock sat in the draughty Ford outside McFarlane's flat until midnight, when the woman left in a taxi. He followed the taxi until it reached the Antonine and then he returned to the station, sat in his chair, put his feet up on his desk, pulled his hat down over his eyes, and went to sleep. He was senior officer on call, but managed to remain like that until 7 a.m.

Elka Willems walked under the dark edifice of the Art Gallery and Museum. The night was still and cold and dark. She was reminded of the time she walked up Buchanan Street and met the man who scarred her for life. It couldn't happen now, though, not tonight, because Phil Hamilton was walking at her side, chatting amiably about his son, Davy, who had just taken his first steps.

Earlier that night there had been another attack in the park. Kimberley Duncan was a pretty twenty-year-old clerical worker and she had been attacked in much the same way as Hazel Hanson. She'd been groped and pawed and was shocked but unhurt. She was unable to say whether her attacker was male or female, but the rest of her description tied in with the description given by Hazel Hanson; youngish, combat jacket, boots. By the time the patrol had responded the park seemed empty; by the time WPC Willems and PC Hamilton had walked around the park for two hours, they were convinced of it. They left the park and walked back to Charing Cross, taking the long route via Gibson Street.

Thursday's dawn nudged Glasgow grudgingly from her sleep; grey light reached down from Beattock summit, caressing her gently from Rutherglen to Bearsden, stroking her long limbs which lay on either side of the river, stirring life into her slumbering heart. The beautiful sleeping bitch woke to a north wind which howled down from the Campsies, biting into every alley, gusting up every stairway and into a million homes. Glasgow clawed and thrashed into life and awoke with a scream.

The screaming kettle woke Ray Sussock. He wiped his eyes and felt itchy and tacky. He went to the lavatory, then rinsed his face in cold water and went back to his office, where Elka Willems was stirring a mug of steaming coffee.

'You look like you've been on duty for a week, Ray,' she said, handing him the mug with one hand and offering the bowl of sugar with the other.

'Who gave you permission to address senior officers by their Christian names, then?' Sussock yawned and spooned sugar into his coffee.

'You did, old man.' Elka Willems smiled. 'Remember, about eighteen months ago, 'Call me Raymond, please, we're off duty now,' She mimicked his rich Gorbals accent.

'All right, all right.' He turned away, still yawning.

'It wasn't until then that I began to fancy you.'

'I said all right.'

'Wassamatter, Raymond?' She hooked a finger under his jacket collar and smiled. 'Don't you feel sexy this morning?'

'Not when I slept in the bed I slept in.'

'At least you slept.'

'So there was nothing to call the duty senior for.'

'Nothing the brave lads in blue couldn't handle.'

'Was it busy?

'Kept us on our toes, but we've had worse right enough.' She took the mug of coffee from Sussock's hands and helped herself to a mouthful. 'Thanks. Well, there was a break-in at a jeweller's in Hillhead, they came down

through the roof, a job for the CID, so it'll come to you as
a neatly typed-up report.'

'That's all we need.' He took a drink of coffee and
offered the mug to Elka Willems. She shook her head.

'A couple of knifings when the dancin' chucked them
out. One's still critical.' She drummed the top of Sussock's
desk with her fingers. 'Oh yes, a lorry-driver from the
Smoke reckoned to save some of his gaffer's money by
overnight parking in a side-street and kipping in the cab.'

'I think I know the rest,' said Sussock, sinking back into
the chair.

'Right. He heard some local neds screwing the rig so he
went out, we think to offer them some money to beat it, so
they bent a jack handle over his skull and continued to
screw the lorry. As far as we could tell they got away with
three crates of apples. The rest was routine; breach of the
peace, drunk and disorderly, stolen motors.'

'It's like seeing a film for the twentieth time.' Sussock
squeezed his eyes with the side of his index finger and his
thumb. 'When I get back to the flat I'm going to sleep
until next week.'

'Not if I'm back before you, old Sussock.' She swung
away, still managing to look devastating in a police
uniform at 7.15 a.m. 'If I get back before you, you have
got to pay a little forfeit before you can sleep.'

'In that case I'm going now.'

'No, you're not. You've got work to do. You received
feedback last night about the Pahl case. It's in your tray.'

'You should have woken me, for Christ's sake!' Sussock
scrambled to his feet.

'Why? There wasn't much to do.'

'That means there's something to do! Bloody Fabian's
in at eight-thirty, you know what he's like.'

'I know, wants everything yesterday, and if something's
not done you just take cover.'

'So why set me up?'

'Who's setting you up? Don't get excited, Raymond, it's not good for your blood pressure. There was only one thing to do and it's on its way from Edinburgh at this moment at the request of Detective-Sergeant Sussock.'

Sussock sat down. Elka Willems leant forward and kissed his forehead.

'Your big problem is that you'll have to wait here to discuss it with Fabian, which means you won't be home before nine-thirty, so I suggest you have a lot of coffee and save your strength for that little forfeit you're going to have to make.' She left his office.

Sussock rested his elbows on the arms of his chair, hung his head and said 'shit!'.

He got to his feet and checked his in-tray. There were two slips of paper. One was a telex message from the Royal Netherlands Police. They had no trace of any of the sets of prints. The Police National Computer print-out was more interesting. It read:

Name: Donald James McArthur   *Age*: 29

Last known address: 12/4 Lochaber St
                        Townhead
                        Glasgow

Also known as: Donald McFarlane, Leadbeater, Smiler.

Previous Convictions: Theft
                          Assault to Severe Injury
                          Assault and Reset

File held by Lothian and Borders Police, W Division.

Sussock was into his second cup of coffee when PC Hamilton knocked on his door. Hamilton had been on duty all night, he was looking tired and his previously neatly ironed shirt was crumpled. With Hamilton was a motor-cycle courier, red waterproof jacket, white helmet, knee-length boots. He held a package under his arm. The biker slipped his helmet off and said, 'Delivery from Lothian and Borders, sir.' He handed Sussock the package and got him to sign for it. The courier left his office together with Hamilton, doubtless, thought Sussock, to go to the canteen. Sussock tore open the package and took out the file.

McFarlane, or McArthur, or whatever his name was, had a thin file. He didn't seem to have generated a great deal of police activity.

Age	Offence	Court	Disposal
18	Theft	Glasgow Sheriff	Admonished
20	Assault to Severe Injury	Glasgow Sheriff	Fined £75
23	Assault and Reset	High Court, Glas	Fined £50 Two years' imprisonment

The file contained statements relevant to each offence that witnesses and McFarlane, or McArthur, had made to the police. Also in the file was a Social Background Report which had evidently been requested in connection with his first conviction.

Social Work Department
Central 10

Report on: Donald McFarlane
              12/4 Lochaber Street
              Townhead
              Glasgow
Age: 18
Court: Glasgow Sheriff
Offence: Theft

Previous Convictions: None known or recorded.

Family and Home Circumstances

Marion McArthur	45 years	Housewife
Donald James McArthur	18 years	Unemployed. Subject of this report.
Geraldine McArthur	14 years	Scholar.

The family home is a sparsely furnished council flat in a high-rise development in the north of the city. The home has a very depressing atmosphere, with only rudimentary furnishings and little decoration. The family income is derived entirely from statutory sources and amounts to £20 per week. Pressing debts to a money-lending company and to the South of Scotland Electricity Board were reported. Mr McArthur contributes £5 per week towards his keep.

Personal History

Mr McArthur appears to have enjoyed a privileged childhood. He spent the first fifteen years of his life living with his family in a large house in Bearsden. He was privately educated and was hoping for a university place. Mr McArthur's father was the owner and managing director of a small but prosperous engineering company. It seems that the company was taken over by an asset-stripping consortium which wrested control from Mr McArthur's father, who began to drink and gamble heavily, cashing in insurance policies and eventually having to sell the family home to pay off his debts. He disappeared shortly after the sale of the house and his body was later washed ashore on the lower reaches of the Clyde. It is presumed he had committed suicide.

Mr McArthur was forced to leave the private school he was attending and he and his mother and sister moved into council accommodation. Mr McArthur could not settle in the local authority school, and left when he was 16 years old with no qualifications. He has had difficulty in finding employment. Shortly after leaving school he spent some six months employed in a small boat-yard in Hampshire where he worked for his keep and a small allowance. He returned to Glasgow when his mother began to suffer a nervous condition and could no longer properly care for Geraldine (then 12 years old). He has remained in Glasgow and has not worked since his return from England, although he has made enquiries about joining the armed forces.

Offence

Mr McArthur entered derelict property and removed a quantity of lead piping. He said that it was his intention to sell the lead in an attempt to ease his financial problems. Mr McArthur informed the writer that he did not appreciate his act was one of theft since the building was going to be demolished. Mr McArthur expressed his regret at the incident.

Conclusion

Mr McArthur impressed as an embittered young man who seems to be socially and intellectually frustrated. He does however seem to be showing responsibility towards his younger sister and does not impress as being of a criminal disposition. The writer respectfully recommends that a deferred sentence be considered as an appropriate disposal in this case.

Simon Mahon
Social Worker

Also in the file was a photocopy of discharge papers from the armed services.

Army Form B 108C

TEMPORARY CERTIFICATE OF DISCHARGE

(Issued to a soldier on leaving the Colours when his CERTIFICATE OF SERVICE is not immediately available)

The bearer

No *28971*   Rank *PTE*   Name *McArthur*

has been released from service with the Colours and is accordingly free to take up civilian employment.

The cause of his discharge:

Defect in enlistment procedure

His military conduct is provisionally assessed as:

EXEMPLARY

Place *Aldershot*

It was stamped:

Headquarters
Depot The Para Regt
and Airborne Forces

According to the charge sheets in the file he had badly damaged someone in a bar brawl only a few days after he was discharged from the army. There was a second assault conviction three years after that, which was part of McArthur's involvement in a fencing operation for which he was also convicted of reset. According to the file the gems were worth £35,000 and McArthur's light sentence indicated he played a small part in the affair. He served eighteen months of the two-year sentence, the first twelve in Barlinnie and the last six in an open prison in Ayrshire. Inside the file were his prison medical records which showed that he suffered from a heart murmur.

Sussock closed the file and clasped his hands together. McArthur had taken a power dive from privilege into the poverty trap. He'd tried to get out via the Armed Forces but had been kicked in the teeth when they found out about his congenital defect and his police record. He had turned to crime and had rounded it all off with a stretch in the slammer. Sussock found himself harbouring a sneaking sympathy for McArthur, and felt he might have done the same thing in those circumstances. Nevertheless, he was left with a young man who despite his heart defect was tough; he was vicious, he was ambitious, and he was clever. He had disappeared for two years following his release from gaol and had suddenly resurfaced, calling himself McFarlane, a wealthy home-owner, car-owner, who took a fur-wrapped floozie to his flat each night and yet who drove a beat-up delivery van by day. Sussock took the file and laid it on Donoghue's desk. It was 8.15 a.m.

In Amsterdam it was 9.15 a.m. It was a cold morning with a fine drizzle blown on a stiff north-easterly wind. Two black Mercedes saloons drove sedately through the early-morning rain towards Schiphol. In the opposite direction the last remnants of the rush-hour traffic was sifting into the city. The Mercedes drove on, in close company, their windscreen wipers beating methodically. In each car sat four men. Each man was dressed in plain clothes, each was armed. When the cars were fourteen kilometres from Amsterdam they reduced speed, turned off the main road and drove towards the small hamlet of Aunspeet. The cars drove on for only another few hundred metres before halting underneath a stand of swaying cypress trees. The windscreens of the cars began to mist over. No one spoke in either of the cars, the only sound being the rain hammering on the roof and the sudden swish of branches tugged in a stronger gust of wind. In front of the cars was a row of houses running down the right-hand side of the road. They were small and brightly painted and most had lights on in the downstairs rooms. On the opposite side of the road was a white-painted cottage standing in a small and neat garden. Further down the road a telephone engineer scaled a telegraph pole. In two black Mercedes eight men flicked off the safety-catches of their automatics and then settled back and waited.

Ann Voegler stood at the window in the kitchen and

looked out across the garden, through the rain, at the two black cars which had drawn up under the trees. They were the first thing that worried her. The second thing that worried her was that the phone was dead, so that she couldn't ring the number she had memorized and was supposed to ring if anything untoward happened. She replaced the receiver, went back to the kitchen and looked at the cars. They weren't moving, and nobody in them seemed to be moving. She let the curtain fall back and ambled to the front room where the children were playing. She was an amiable and shapeless woman who looked older than her forty-seven years, and generally she was happy. On the morning of Thursday, 4th November she was not happy because she was suspicious.

Ann Voegler's suspicions were confirmed when her front door was kicked open just as a man burst through the back door at about the same time as someone threw a brick through an upstairs window. Suddenly the cottage was full of men running at her from every direction. One pushed her against the wall and held a gun to her head. Two more ran upstairs, two others grabbed the children and ran out towards the cars. Ann Voegler was too frightened to scream.

The 'Sea-Food, Mama' restaurant was an exclusive eats joint, set among some small and exclusive shops in Hampstead. It was raided by the Metropolitan Police at dawn on 4th November. The report, filed later, detailed opposition being 'subdued by truncheons' and the 'sniffer' dogs pawing frantically at a safe in the manager's office.

Donoghue closed the file. 'What do you think, Ray?'
   'Pretty well confirms what we already thought, sir.'
   'Uh-huh.' Donoghue flicked his lighter, the tobacco in his pipe began to glow and blue smoke began to drift towards the ceiling. It was his first pipe of the day and

Sussock knew Donoghue would be surrounded by smoke for the next eight hours. Donoghue cleared his throat. 'So where do we go from here, Ray?'

Ray Sussock didn't know. He didn't want to know. He was a detective-sergeant, Donoghue was a detective-inspector, he was fifty-four years old, Donoghue had just edged into his forties, he was tired, Donoghue was fresh. Right then Sussock didn't know where to go from here, nor was he overly concerned. He replied by looking at Donoghue wearily.

Donoghue grunted and glanced at his watch. 'Well, by now Heer Van der Veeght's colleagues ought to have rescued the Pahl child and that swish eating-house in London ought to have been busted, the news of which may reach McFarlane's ears quite soon, if he's involved. In which case he may be panicked into a move. He'll have to be watched, Ray.'

'Yes, sir.'

There was a sharp, frantic rap on Donoghue's office door. Sussock turned, Donoghue said 'come in'. Montgomerie pushed open the door. He looked anxious.

'I think you should see this, sir.' He held up the leather-bound notebook which had been found in Dominique Pahl's house. Inside the notebook were some larger sheets of paper.

'Translated it all at last have you, Montgomerie?'

'Last night, sir. Only broke the code last night.'

'What is it, then?' Donoghue took his pipe from his mouth and cradled the bowl in his right hand.

'The book is a sort of address book. The writing which the Dutchman and I found with the photographs is a statement.'

'Which makes interesting reading?'

'Very, sir.'

'Good. What are your movements today, Montgomerie?'

'Surveillance of Gavin Floyd, the councillor.'

'Ah, yes. Well, better get on with it then, eh?'

'Yes, sir.' Montgomerie laid the book on Donoghue's desk and quietly left the room.

'And you, Ray? Tired?'

'A wee bit,' conceded Sussock.

'Well, thanks for staying late. Away you go.' Sussock stood sluggishly and left the room.

Donoghue sat back in his chair, put his pipe in his mouth and looked at the two items on his desk. He picked up the McArthur/McFarlane file and read through it again. Like Sussock, he had an uncomfortable feeling of danger from McFarlane, but unlike Sussock he could muster no sympathy for the man.

Inside the leather-bound notebook were six sheets of foolscap paper on which was writing in English, and in a neat hand. The first thing that Donoghue noticed was that the handwriting was not Montgomerie's; it was a round, full, female hand. Donoghue didn't dwell upon this observation but put his pipe down upon his desk top and began to read:

Soon I am going to be murdered.

I want to write about my life with Frans. I have nothing to lose but it helps me to know that this is hidden. They may search the house and are more likely to pass over a book of numbers than a book of words.

I married Frans five years ago. He was a house-painter and also ran a second-hand book store. His mother was a Malay and his father was a Dutchman. We lived in Rotterdam. Sometimes Frans would be away from home for days. Always he seemed tense and frightened. We had a child, a girl, we called her Dominique.

One day Frans came home. He was shaking. He told me to pack some things and get our passports. We drove in our little car to Denmark where we got a ferry to Norway. On the boat Frans told me about the Triad.

It is run by Malaysians who import heroin from the East and distribute it in Europe. Frans had worked in it for a long time. Now he tried to leave. But you can't leave. So we ran for his life. In Scandinavia we were very obvious, the three of us travelling in our odd little car.

They found us and took us back to Holland. They killed Frans. I will not tell you how, it is too horrible. They took my child and told me that I will work for the Triad.

I came to Glasgow to live in this big house. Each month I go to a shed in the docks and collect a shipment of prawns. I collect the boxes with a red label. I take them back to the house and a van comes to collect them and take them, I think, to London. On the side of the van is written 'Sea-Food, Mama Restaurant, Hampstead'. Sometimes I have to put up a guest, always an oriental man. Once every two months I receive a photograph of Dominique. The man who owns the shed in the docks is a nice old man. I do not think he is connected with the Triad. The other man is connected with the Triad. It was he who killed my husband in Amsterdam. I think his name is McFarlane. I was worried about him. He is ruthless and ambitious. For a long time I knew he wanted me out of the way.

It will be useless to talk to my visitor when he comes. They want an example. It will be useless to tell him that McFarlane sabotaged the shipment. After I am dead someone will come and talk with McFarlane and he will assume my place but they will not use this house. As soon as I received the phone call I went to the police. But I realized if they did not kill me they would probably kill Dominique. The leather book contains addresses of people connected with the Triad. They are not holders of important positions.

D.P.

Donoghue didn't look at the rest of the foolscap sheets on which were the decoded addresses. 'Poor cow,' he said to himself and lit his pipe. He tried to steady his hand but couldn't control the trembling.

Montgomerie thought that he could tail either Councillor Floyd or Charles Stuart, but all roads leading to Rome, and a Regional Councillor being likely to have less hectic a day than a businessman, he decided to follow Floyd. He had checked out the council business agenda and had found that Floyd was holding a surgery in the Council Chambers from 9.30 a.m., Thursday 4th. He relaxed his tone, unbuttoned his coat, unclipped his tie and slipped it into his pocket. Then he shuffled across George Square and into the Council Chambers. The Chambers were impressive, elegant; graceful stairways and a vast marble floor. A commissionaire stood by a highly polished desk near the door.

'Want to see Councillor Floyd,' said Montgomerie to the commissionaire.

'You need an appointment,' replied the man, not trying to hide his distaste. He knew the type: unemployed from the schemes, come to make their demands. 'Do you have an appointment?'

'No.'

'You need an appointment.' the commissionaire half turned away. He seemed ex-military, late-middle-aged, white cap, blue serge uniform, white bandolier, shoes you could eat a dinner off.

'It's urgent,' said Montgomerie.

The commissionaire picked up the phone on his desk and sighed in the exasperated way Montgomerie had long since identified as the hallmark of petty officials under pressure. The man spoke into the phone, listened, thanked the person at the other end and replaced the receiver.

'There's no more appointments today, laddie,' he said, not looking at Montgomerie and pretending to sort some papers. 'Councillor Floyd's surgery finishes at ten-thirty. He's got his last appointment in now.'

Montgomerie said, 'Thank you very much.'

It was 10.28.

Montgomerie pushed his way through the revolving doors, crossed the street between the ornamental lamps, and stood next to the war memorial in George Square. He buttoned up his coat, clipped on his tie, lit a cigarette and waited. The councillors who had been holding surgeries came out of the Chambers together, looking like a bunch of hoods from a 1930s gangster flick. On the pavement they formed a half-circle with their hands shoved deep into their coat pockets, all looking flushed with self-importance at being one of the gang. Montgomerie thought he could fancy being a councillor, picking up fat expenses cheques and achieving political gain just by lending a sympathetic ear, and leaving it up to young girls in blue jeans with second-hand motors to shovel the crap.

The smug bunch stood chatting for a couple of minutes before splitting up. A large proportion of the group ambled towards the café area on Ingram Street, two hurried off in the direction of the multi-storey car-park on George Street, and Gavin Floyd splintered solo. He waved an arm to the group and walked on to George Square, passing by Montgomerie, who buried his face behind a hastily struck match. Floyd walked across the square and up St Vincent Street.

Montgomerie followed close behind as Floyd walked in the crowds, falling back as the pavements emptied in the further reaches of St Vincent Street. The councillor walked briskly; he had short legs and took rapid, hurried steps, keeping his left hand in his coat pocket but swinging his right arm vigorously. He walked to the brow and down into Charing Cross. He crossed over the motorway and, out of the grid system, drove a roughly south-westerly path through the side-streets towards the Broomielaw and the river. He had been walking for half an hour and he had reached that part of the city where the streets are narrow, where the wind blows the paper along the pavement, where kids play on the cobbles, and where the air is heavy with dust from the sandblasted tenements. Floyd walked through the streets. It was just the back of eleven and the publicans were unlocking the steel doors and carrying out the empty kegs.

It was another ten minutes before Montgomerie knew Floyd was making for the Bells of Hell. The Bells of Hell began life as a stone-built customs shed standing at the entrance to a quay where black liners with tall stacks took on immigrants for the New World. That was in the early part of the century when the river had a big life. After the second war the building fell into disuse, pigeons got into the loft, and weeds got into the basement and grew on the quay. For many years the building, roughly conical in shape, stood empty. Neglected, it passed from the state of being 'in need of repair' to 'extensive renovations required', and only when it had stood completely derelict for ten years was it bought by a city businessman. He repointed the stonework, put some windows into the sloping upper walls, and gradually turned the building into one of the most expensive and most hedonistic clubs in the city. Membership was by individual negotiation backed with references requested in telephone numbers. The quay was never fully cleared of weeds, and it became a stamp of social achievement among a handful of the city's chic to arrive at a party a little drunk, and with the odd seed-pod stuck to your Guccis.

The councillor walked along the quay, negotiating the parked cars and stepping over the occasional weed. He walked near the edge of the quay, often with just a hastily built wall between him and the Clyde. The stiff breeze buffeted his coat and tugged at his hair as he walked, outlined against the grey skies forming over Dunoon. Floyd walked up to the door, a heavy metal object with a skull and crossbones emblazoned upon it, and rang the bell. Montgomerie watched from a hundred yards away, leaning against a white Mercedes. Floyd looked small against the building. The steel door swung outwards, Floyd rummaged in his coat pocket and then held something up, evidently for inspection by a man whom Montgomerie could not see. Floyd entered the building and the door was pulled shut behind him.

Montgomerie crossed directly across the car-park, through the weeds, went up to the door and pressed the bell. An extractor fan was pushing warm air out to the right of the door. On the river a small Soviet freighter nudged its way gently towards Greenock. Montgomerie pressed the bell again. The door was pushed open by a joker who was just this side of giant status and whose face Montgomerie vaguely recognized from somewhere: a brawl in a quarter-gill when he was in uniform maybe, or a face that leapt out at him when he was leafing through the mugshots. It was a scarred face with heavy cheeks and a broken nose. It leaned down towards Montgomerie and said, 'You a member, sir?'

'No,' said Montgomerie, 'but I'm coming in.'

'You can't come in if you're not a member, sir.' The man stood up. He was six and a half feet if he was an inch.

'You reckon?'

'I reckon.' The man leaned forward to pull the door shut. 'If you're not in, you're not in, Jim.'

'Will this get me in?' Montgomerie flashed his ID quickly and then put it back inside his jacket. 'Or maybe you want to go back inside for obstructing a police officer. Out on licence, aren't you?'

'You didn't say you was the Bill.' The man's hand

slipped from the door.

'You know now. Do I get in?'

The man stood aside.

'You want to see the head man?'

Montgomerie shook his head.

'That old guy that just came in, he comes here a lot, eh?'

'Mr Floyd? Yeah he's a big day-time customer, is Mr Floyd. Talks with the other businessmen at lunchtimes. Some lunch, lasts for three hours, sometimes more, they're too steamboats to walk when they're done, the businessmen. I'm just waiting for the day one of them drives his Bentley into the river—that little wall's got no foundation, you could kick it over. But Mr Floyd, yeah, once, twice, three times a week for his lunch, but then he usually doesn't pick up the bill. See me, I have a mug of tea and a cheese piece in the back room and only half an hour to eat it in, but this is the only job I can get on account of my form.'

'Starting over's tough,' said Montgomerie.

'I'm doin' all right. Been here a year already.'

'Keep it up,' replied Montgomerie and walked down a carpeted corridor with a curved roof, towards the receptionist. She was a pretty girl in a small black skirt and sheer tights. She was sitting at a desk in an alcove and behind her were racks of coats. She smiled at Montgomerie with the same insincere welcome developed to perfection by air hostesses. She handed him a gold-plated ballpoint and pushed a book forward. Montgomerie took the pen and looked at the book. It was a conventional visitors' book in which the patrons signed only their name followed by a six-figure number. He signed:

S. Holmes 221999

The girl took the pen and turned the book round and said 'Good to see you again, Mr Holmes.'

'Nice to be back,' replied Montgomerie, peeling off his coat. The girl stood and took the coat, continuing to smile at him, spiky black eyelashes, and brilliant, brittle teeth flashing in the gloom.

'Oh,' said Montgomerie and fished his wallet from his jacket. He took a pound note and offered it to the girl, whose smile faltered.

'I'm sorry, Mr Holmes, the charge went up six months ago.'

Montgomerie raised his eyebrows. 'I've been overseas,' he said.

'It's an extra fifty pence now, sir.' The girl regained her smile.

Montgomerie dipped into his pocket and gave her a fifty-pence piece.

'Total security guaranteed, sir,' she said, and handed Montgomerie a white tab.

'That right?'

'Oh yes. We're very careful here, sir.'

The corridor towards the dining area and bar was more thickly carpeted, the walls were white-plastered and the roof was lower. The corridor ended in a large dim room, split between a dining area which took up two-thirds of the floor space, and the slightly elevated cocktail bar. The two areas were segregated by pine uprights and leafy plants. The roof could not be seen. Young, slim women dressed in white blouses, black mini-skirts, fishnet tights and high heels carried trays or pushed trolleys. All seemed to have smiles frozen to their faces. A few men sat in the dining area, a few more heads were visible in the cocktail bar. Montgomerie half closed his eyes in an attempt to penetrate the gloom and, sweeping from left to right, located Floyd sitting at a dining-table with another man. A plastic doll with swaying hips walked up to Montgomerie.

'Can I help you, sir?' she asked smoothly through her smile.

'I'm meeting a friend for dinner,' he said. 'I'd like a drink while I wait.'

'Very good, sir, if you'd like to step this way.' She swung neatly on her heels and led him to the cocktail bar. She showed him to a seat under the wall.

'I'll sit over by the plants,' he said. 'So I can see my friend.'

'I'll escort your friend to you, sir. If you'd like to tell me his name.' The smile became more forced.

Despite his looks, his pick of girls, one of Montgomerie's problems had been an inability to resist charmers. It wasn't until his final year at university that he had first resisted such a girl, and in doing so experienced an odd but pleasant sense of victory.

'I'll sit by the plants,' he said to the long-legged woman. 'And I'd like a half-pint of lager.'

'Yes, sir,' she said, and walked to the bar. Montgomerie noticed a trace of anger in her step.

He sat at a table by a leafy plant and was not surprised to discover that the plant was synthetic.

He thought the Bells of Hell was just an upmarket version of the modern Glasgow bars, soft, comfortable, no clocks, no natural light, designed to lull punters into a sense of dreamlike unreality, all to aid the process of filling the till with cash.

He bent one of the leaves back so that he could see better across the dining area. He could make out Floyd sitting with another man, both sitting side-on to Montgomerie. The other man was well dressed; expensive blue suit, a blue-striped shirt and a fancy tie done up in a big knot. His hair was greased and reflected the light from the bulb on their table. They were leaning forward, talking intently.

The smile with legs brought his lager on a brass tray

over which a white cloth was draped. She put the glass of lager on the table in front of Montgomerie.

'That'll be two pounds, please, sir,' she said sullenly.

'Two quid?'

'Yes, sir.'

Montgomerie took the money from his wallet and wondered how he was going to explain an expenses claim for seventy-per-cent of a Duke of Wellington, itemized as one drink and the hire of a coat hanger. He handed the money to the woman but grabbed her wrist as she took it. She let out a stifled cry and Montgomerie released his grip slightly.

'I want you to sit down,' he said.

'Please, we're not allowed to fraternize with the customers.'

'Sit!'

'Please, all I have to do is call one of the heavies, I'll meet you outside if you let me go.'

'Just plant your beautiful flesh on that seat.' He squeezed her wrist and the woman pivoted and sank on to the chair opposite Montgomerie. 'If I let your wrist go will you not make a noise or try to leave that seat?' He spoke slowly and carefully, looking at her intently. She nodded and Montgomerie released her wrist. She rubbed it with her other hand. 'What do you see through the plants?'

'Men sitting eating.'

'Good. Those two men sitting there in the middle of the floor, the old guy with glasses and the younger smoothed-up version, see them?'

'Aye.'

'Good. Keep looking at them. Know them?'

'One. Mr Stuart.'

'He's the smoothie, right?'

'Aye.'

'See him often?'

' 'Most every evening, sometimes in the day as well, like now.'

'Always eats with other people?'

'Aye.'

'What sort of other people?'

'Men. Look, who are you?'

'Later. What about the other guy? Seen him before?'

'I can't make him out, it's too dim.'

'It's bright enough.'

'All right, yes, I've seen him in here before, usually during the day. I don't know his name, though.'

'Seen him with Mr Stuart before?'

'Couple of times. Why?'

The blue-suited man leaned back, smiled and took a paper parcel from his jacket and put it on the table. Floyd picked it up and pocketed it.

'Did you see that?' hissed Montgomerie.

'Aye. So what? Mr Stuart often gives people money like that.'

'How do you know it's money?'

'What else could it be?'

'OK. I'll need your name and address, hen,' said Montgomerie.

'Why?'

'Because I'm a police officer and you may have just witnessed a serious crime.' He took out his notebook and ballpoint.

'I thought you might be the polis somehow,' she said bitterly.

'Why, been in trouble, have you?'

'Let's just say I crossed paths with the boys in blue on a couple of occasions. It isn't peaches and cream that brings a girl to a joint like this, there's hard knocks behind those smiles.' Her own smile had gone.

'Name, hen?'

'Sylvia McElroy, c/o Jones Guest House, Great Western

Road, age 32, previous convictions for opportuning, one five-year-old daughter—illegitimate, of course; past: no breaks; present: one day at a time; future: bleak.' She got up from the chair and walked towards the bar.

Montgomerie shut his notebook and pocketed it. He sipped the lager and turned again to look at Floyd and Stuart. Then he saw a third man approach the table and Montgomerie's heart seemed to explode. He recognized the third man; he'd followed him home one night, he'd searched his home with its weird decorations. The newcomer shook hands with Floyd and Stuart and sat at their table.

He was Donald McFarlane. (or McArthur. Or Smiler. Or Leadbeater.)

CHAPTER 8

It was a small room, twelve feet by twelve feet, with green tiled walls up to about four feet from the ground, from where it was white plaster to the ceiling. There was a single bulb without a shade hanging from the ceiling. High on one wall was a small window. On the floor was a sheet of thick industrial linoleum, one table and two chairs. It was a room with no distractions, a crude, clinical design to focus attention on the matter in hand. It was an interview room.

'Sorry to have kept you, Mr Floyd.' Montgomerie sat down and smiled. He put a manilla envelope on the table.

'You said a minute. Two bloody hours isn't a minute.'

'I had to attend to a few things. I'm sure the constable kept you company.' Montgomerie glanced at Hamilton.

'Him! He didn't say a bloody word.'

Hamilton stood against the wall, arms folded in front of him, still, impassive.

'He's not supposed to.'

'Does he have to stay here?'

'Uh-huh.' Montgomerie leaned back on his chair and smiled. 'Why?'

'He bothers me.'

'Why?'

'Just standing there saying nothing.'

'He's a witness.'

'Your witness?'

'And yours.'

'I don't understand.'

'Well, he's a witness that the statement you are going to make is made voluntarily and without you being subject to threats or duress. If, however, I do lose my temper and bounce your head on the floor a couple of times, then he could be very useful to your action against the police.'

'You wouldn't do that!'

'Scottish criminal law requires a witness, "two independent streams of evidence" or whatever it is, I can't remember.'

'He's independent?'

'Very.'

'Who is he?'

'Police Constable P246 Hamilton, Philip.'

'I don't like him here. Where does it say in law there's got to be a witness?'

'There's no legislation; it's part of the common law. Most of Scotland's law is based on the common law and very few criminal acts are codified in statute; did you know that? We prosecute for murder under the common law.'

'I haven't killed anybody.'

'It was only by way of example.'

'You've no right to frighten. You said something about duress.'

'I'm not trying to frighten you. Why are you here?'

'Because . . .'

'Yes?'

'Well . . . well, because you and your mates kicked my door down and dragged me down the close and into the van. I seen my arms, you marked me, dragging me backwards down the stairs.'

'We asked you to come quietly. We didn't kick your door down.'

'Damn near.' Montgomerie had long noticed that it was in the interview rooms that a person's real self showed, the sixteen-year-olds who didn't give and showed themselves to be men of real mettle, the women who babbled like schoolgirls, the councillor who sat askew on the chair, like a sullen child, half lifting his head as he talked, exaggerating to justify his indignation. 'You splintered the wood round the lock.'

'No, we didn't.'

'Bloody did.'

Montgomerie let it ride.

'You really doing me for breach of the peace?' asked Floyd after a few moments of silence.

'Uh-huh. Already written down the charge. On the fourth of November in the afternoon in the vicinity of Glamis Causeway, Easterhouse you did shout, bawl, curse and swear and did commit a breach of the peace.'

'I wasn't screaming loud.'

'You were making enough racket to gather a crowd. Mind you, I tend to think they were more interested in the subject of the arrest rather than the reason for it.'

'Aye, and that's another thing, why did you come in the early evening, people and kids in the streets then, fine headline, eh, "Councillor arrested for breach of the peace, and neighbours look on".'

'I reckon that's the least of your problems.'

'What do you mean by that?' Again the slight jerk of the head.

'Well, how about Councillor Gavin Floyd, chairman of the Roads and Highways committee, regular contacts with a shady outfit called Torvaney-Stuart, regular deposits into his bank account over and above his regular income.'

'You haven't been at my bank account!'

'Like to bet?' Montgomerie patted the envelope. 'We photocopied your current account statements for the last thirty-six months, and the statements from your deposit account since you opened it a year ago.'

'The bank manager's a personal friend of mine!' Floyd spluttered. 'We exchange cards at Christmas.'

'He was. He's feeling pretty sick right now. In fairness he wasn't keen to let us have the details we wanted and so we had to wave a warrant under his nose. Anyway, there's a little matter of two thousand pounds to discuss. It seems to have come into your accounts in dribs and drabs over the last three years, since you've been chairman of the Roads and Highways committee, in fact.'

Floyd sank a heavily lined face into a pudgy, short-fingered hand. His grey hair glistened. 'Two thousand pounds,' he whispered.

'Give or take a hundred. Hardly worth it, was it, Gavin? Would you like to make a statement?'

'No,' he said, raising his head in that way he had. 'No, I wouldn't like to make a statement. I'd like a cigarette.'

'No statement, no fag.'

'That a fact?'

' 'S a fact' said Montgomerie. 'It's a fact like lunches in the Bells of Hell and a character called McFarlane. We're very interested in McFarlane. You can work for yourself, Gavin, or you can work against yourself; I suggest you do the former, and you can start by telling us what you know about McFarlane.'

'What's wrong with Mr McFarlane?'

'What were you talking about?'

'We were talking business.' He tried to sound important but it didn't quite come off.

'Do tell,' said Montgomerie drily.

'Legitimate business. He wanted a backer for a business deal.'

'Tell me.'

'Why? He's a pleasant young man is Mr McFarlane. He's got class, you know, went to a private school.'

'That's important, is it? That's the sort of company you want to move with, is it? Like being on Christmas-card terms with your bank manager. Getting tired of good old G 34, are you?'

'I'm ambitious. I've worked hard all my days and got nothing to show for it. I've got fifteen or even twenty good years left, I'd like a nest egg for my retirement. I don't want to have money problems when I'm seventy. Young Mr McFarlane has a good business proposition.'

'Tell me about it.'

'Na!'

'Shall I guess?'

'If you want.'

'Would it be a transportation system, perhaps?'

Floyd's eyes widened. He nodded. Montgomerie waited.

'He has this idea,' said Floyd. 'A good one. Light express parcel deliveries, Glasgow to London each night, deliveries in inner London the following morning. He reckons there's a lot of companies in the Glasgow area that need to send time-sensitive documents to the Smoke faster than the GPO can manage, and they'll pay for the service if it's less than sending their own courier. They deliver to our collecting point before, say, 8 p.m., and we deliver in the Smoke the next morning. He wants a backer.'

'Sounds good,' said Montgomerie.

'Why did you think it was a transportation proposition?'

'Because his last system was lost when a fashionable munchies joint was raided this morning.'

'This morning!'

'Found out about it pretty quickly,' said Montgomerie, more to himself than Floyd. 'When did you arrange to meet McFarlane?'

'Charlie Stuart telephoned me this morning. About nine o'clock. I don't understand.'

'There's been a lot of rapid telegraphy,' said Montgomerie. 'But McFarlane's scheme, it's a good idea, it might even work, it might be just the thing you need to get a nest-egg: two main areas of concern.' Montgomerie held up his index finger. 'One, the money you want to invest is money taken as bribes to favour tenders submitted by Torvaney-Stuart.'

'That's a lie!'

'Wait, we'll come on to that. The other big area of concern,' said Montgomerie, holding up a second finger, 'is that once a month you'll be taking goods other than legitimate parcels . . .'

'There was no suggestion—'

'—Of anything underhand? I'm sure there wasn't. I think I just saved you from getting mixed up in a really nasty set-up. Let me tell you something about Mr McFarlane.'

'I wish you would. He had excellent references.'

'Who from, your pal Stuart? We both know how crooked he is, don't we?'

Floyd paled slightly. 'He seemed an OK guy, Mr McFarlane.'

'They all do when they want to help you get rid of your money. You get-rich-quick merchants slay me, you all find out there's no quick way, you find out the hard way, and yet you go on believing there's pots of gold just sitting around waiting to be picked up.'

'Don't,' said Floyd.

'Don't what?'

'Don't believe that.'

'Jesus,' sighed Montgomerie. He leaned forward and took a packet of cigarettes from his jacket pocket. He offered one to Floyd. 'Forget what I said earlier about no fags, Gavin,' he said, 'let's start fresh.'

Floyd took a cigarette greedily. Or was it anxiously? Montgomerie banked on anxiety; after all, he had kept him waiting for two hours just to build up his anxiety level. He struck a match and held it out. Floyd leaned forward and cupped his hands round the flame. His fingers were trembling.

'Spent time out of doors, have you?' asked Montgomerie, lighting his own cigarette.

'Aye, why?'

'I wondered why you put your hands round the flame just then, there's no draught in here.'

'Don't miss much, do you?'

'Not a great deal.'

'Aye, I've spent most my working life out doors. National Service, Shipyards, Docks.'

'Seen a bit of life.'

'More than most.'

'What was your National Service?'

'Army.'

'See any action?'

'Korea.'

'That right?'

'That's right. Argyll and Sutherland Highlanders. That's where I first learned to light up in the wind, at twenty below in a gale. I could get it first time.'

'You have something in common with McFarlane.'

'How? The army?'

'No, the mystic east. I was telling you about McFarlane. First off, McFarlane's not his real handle, it's one of his aliases. I won't tell you what the others are. He

was born with a silver spoon in his mouth but while he was
still a teenager he fell from grace with meteoric splendour
and ended up in a council flat with his widowed mother
and little sister. He spent some time in the army, in the
paras, so he's tough as well. Then he got into bother with
the law, that's us, and copped a two-year stretch. So
already your well-spoken young man with good ideas and
references who is looking for a backer, has no money of
his own and is as bent as your pal Stuart.'

The colour drained from Floyd's face.

'It doesn't stop there. In fact, it gets better.'
Montgomerie drew on his cigarette. 'After his spell inside
he disappeared, but we now know he was over in Holland
getting in with some very nasty persons and killing people
by forcing water into their mouths until it burst through
their stomach.'

Floyd's head sagged.

'The man's wife was looking on at the time. McFarlane
had got in with a bunch of oriental gents called a Triad.
They push heroin in Europe, and send it to England
through Glasgow and probably a few other places as well.
It doesn't stop here, thank God. We're a transit point, a
staging-post. The stuff used to come in boxes of frozen
prawns and was shipped to London in a van belonging to
some fancy eating-place. But we busted that, so they'll set
up another operation such as an express delivery of time-
sensitive documents.'

Montgomerie paused and leaned back in his chair.
Floyd sat with his head in his hands. Hamilton stood with
his arms folded in front of him.

'Once back in Scotland, McFarlane operated as small
fry in the poisoned prawns op, and has lately been seen in
the company of a lady who arrived from Holland a few
hours before another lady—who was the widow of the
man McFarlane murdered in Amsterdam—was herself
murdered. This second lady left a statement, in code. She

reckoned McFarlane set her up to advance his own career with ye Triad. Ambitious man, Mr McFarlane, dangerously, ruthlessly, ambitious.' Montgomerie drew the cigarette smoke deep into his lungs. It came out in little clouds as he spoke. 'So you're being attacked on four fronts, Councillor. You're already charged with Breach of the Peace, we've got enough already to send a report to the Procurator Fiscal to warrant a charge of fraud, there's accessory to murder and finally, conspiracy in the sale of dangerous drugs.' He stubbed out his cigarette and picked up his ballpoint. 'Let's tidy up the fraud, shall we, before we get on to the meat? When did Stuart approach you?'

Floyd made no reply.

'Councillor . . .'

There was still no reply and then, suddenly, Montgomerie realized the man was weeping.

Van der Veeght stood at the window of Donoghue's office and looked out on to Charing Cross. A fine drizzle was falling and the people on Sauchiehall Street huddled against the buildings as they walked. He turned and looked at Donoghue, smart in his three-piece suit with a hunter's chain slung across his waistcoat; at his pipe, the blue smoke rising with the convection currents. On the desk in front of Donoghue was a silver coffee-pot, two empty cups and a translation of Dominique Pahl's statement.

'It is not enough,' said Van der Veeght, walking back to the desk and resuming his seat in front of Donoghue.

'It's slim, but it's all we can offer.'

'It's too slim. For a warrant of extradition you need more than that.' He tapped the file on Donoghue's desk. 'A dead woman's statement, coded, is not good enough. She didn't even sign it. It would not satisfy Dutch authorities, but first we have to satisfy your authorities, the Magistrates at Bow Street Court in London, I believe?'

'That's right. They hear all British extradition cases.' Donoghue pulled on his pipe and then took it from his mouth. 'All right, we need something else. The bastard's up to no good, we know he is; even without Dominique Pahl's statement he appears in all the wrong places.'

'I know, you develop a . . . a . . .' Van der Veeght made a circular gesture with his hands.

Donoghue smiled at the big Dutchman. 'A knack,' he said.

'Ja, a knack for smelling bandits.'

'You're right. We both know he's a villain, but we lack the proof.'

'Perhaps we should bring him in for interrogation, lean on him a little.'

Donoghue shook his head. 'It's a ploy right enough, but I don't like it. You stand to lose a lot because you put them on their guard, especially if they're fly, like our friend McFarlane.'

'Fly?'

'Clever, shrewd.' Donoghue blew a plume of smoke towards the ceiling. 'No, when we move for this boy we have to have proof positive. This is the sort of operation that we can sit back and watch for months without acting.'

'I think not, I think if you act quickly you will stop Glasgow becoming a port of entry for heroin.'

'For a few months.'

'You are a pessimist.'

'I'm a realist.'

Van der Veeght let it go.

'You see,' said Donoghue, taking his pipe from his mouth and examining the bowl. 'There is no real time pressure; we've smashed their transit system. If McFarlane wants to take over the Glasgow operation he hasn't done so yet, he hasn't yet set up his own system. All he does is to take his fancy bit of stuff to his flat each night.'

'Do you still have a surveillance on him?'

'Aye. Just from the time he knocks off at the warehouse to the time his moll takes a taxi back to the Antonine.'

'No change in his routine?'

'None. And it doesn't look like he's set to bump anybody off. That's why I say there's no time pressure. Last winter we had a psychopath on the loose, he put us under time pressure because he was knocking his victims down like flies, one a night almost. We had to act then and I nearly lost an officer.'

'I think you are dragging your feet.'

'I think that that's an impertinent remark.'

Van der Veeght stared at Donoghue and then averted his gaze.

'Circle your prey, Heer Van der Veeght, close in steadily. If you rush at him like a bull elephant you'll lose him.'

'I think we should put the cat in with the pigeons.'

'You'll lose everything and I won't allow it.'

'You are not helping me get him back to Holland.'

'You are not assisting me to cope with heroin trafficking, about which I know precious little.'

Both men fell silent and looked away from each other. The only sounds were the footfalls in the corridor outside the office, the clicking of the thermostats on the radiators and the pattering of the rain on the window.

'Perhaps,' said Donoghue slowly, 'you should examine the period when he was in Holland for your additional evidence.'

Van der Veeght looked up. 'Yes, yes, Inspector—the statement, you remember the statement from the man who was turning evidence, the man who saw the one-armed man being murdered.'

'My God, yes!' Donoghue sat upright.

'If he will testify, if he will identify him in court, then with Dominique Pahl's statement we have a murder conviction.'

'Proof positive.'

'I will wire McFarlane's photograph to my headquarters and they will approach the man.'

'When will you get a reply?'

'It depends on the man co-operating. Maybe tomorrow, maybe the day after.'

'We'll keep our eye on him,' Donoghue sighed. 'It'll still be touch and go with their worships in Bow Street. You'll have to convince them that your man isn't fingering just anybody to get a reduced sentence.'

'Sometimes I wonder why I go on, banging my head off the wall.'

'Depressing, isn't it, all the work that goes out of the window because of a legal technicality, or insufficient evidence. Perhaps you should seek promotion, get yourself a senior post where you can get away from the coal-face and let yourself run to fat while spending your time theorizing and bickering about policy.'

'I'd miss the action.'

'You'd miss the comradeship more,' said Donoghue. 'That's what I found after they put me behind this—' he patted his grey steel desk—'I was pleased at first; I'd come a long way in a short time, but then I noticed that all my support came from above or below and not from the side any more. If you lead a team you can't be part of it, and you still take it home to your family each day. You any family?'

'Myself and my wife.'

'No children?'

'Not yet. I am a little old for children, already I am thirty-eight, but my wife is very young so there is still time. Yourself?'

'Wife and two children. A boy and a girl. Our home is in Edinburgh.'

'You are indeed blessed, and to live in Edinburgh. I have seen photographs of the city, it is very beautiful. But such a way to travel each day.'

'Forty miles. A lot of people do it, forty-five minutes by road or rail. You must come and have dinner with us before you leave.'

'I would like that. But for the moment we have business. I will Telex the request now. I think there is a good chance that we should get a reply by Thursday, tomorrow.'

'Tomorrow is Friday, Heer Van der Veeght,' said Donoghue.

'So,' said the Dutchman.

'You've wrung me dry,' said Floyd, wiping his handkerchief under his nose. 'I don't know nothing else.'

'This is enough to keep my boss happy,' replied Montgomerie, leafing through the statement. 'This is your statement which you made half an hour ago. I've had it typed up and I'd like you to read it.' He turned the statement round and pushed it towards Floyd. 'If it's a true record of what you said I'd like you to sign it.' He handed Floyd a ballpoint. Floyd read the statement through silently and then slowly wrote his name at the bottom. 'You've ruined my life,' he said.

'You ruined your own life,' said Montgomerie, taking back the pen and the statement.

'I'll never claw it back, I've lost my job, my position on the council, everything.'

'Cigarette?' Montgomerie held out a packet. Floyd took one and held it between his lips while Montgomerie lit up a match. This time Floyd didn't cup his hands round the flame but gripped the edge of the table. His knuckles were white and the back of his hands mottled.

Montgomerie thought it was a hell of a time of life for a guy to start a prison sentence.

'You're not going to have one yourself?' Floyd sounded frightened.

'No.' Montgomerie slipped the packet back inside his jacket pocket. 'Would you respect a policeman who smoked while he charged you?'

Van der Veeght walked slowly back to the hotel. It was 10.30 on Thursday night, and the city was in the pre-closing-time lull. He was worried about the point Donoghue had made, that even the statement from the man in gaol in Holland might not be enough to satisfy the Bow Street Magistrates into granting permission to extradite McFarlane. The more he thought, the more he believed that he had to stir up a hornets' nest, like he would if he was playing bowls in his home town, knocking the other bowls out of the way if the jack was obscured. In the bar of the Antonine he bought another brandy and then went up to his room. He picked up the phone by the bed and asked the operator for the international dialling code for Rotterdam. She told him that it was 010 3110.

The future doesn't augur well for the area around Helensburgh. The Royal Naval base at Faslane and the next loch west being Holy Loch, where the Americans keep dark secrets, mean that, in the event of a nuclear attack, or a nuclear accident, which the Americans with a criminal degree of understatement call 'a broken arrow', the area north and south of the Clyde including the entire city of Glasgow will be reduced to n square miles of gently undulating ash. Where n is a large positive number. For the present, however, the area continues to act as a magnet for the wealthy who can afford to buy a house where the estuary forges a sharp left-hander between purple hills and pine forests. Some buy the solid stone houses once owned by the whisky barons, others move into luxury bungalows built in the Roman style with arches and pillars. Charles Stuart, Managing Director of Torvaney-Stuart Ltd, was one who could sleep easy while knowing that there was a clutch of hydrogen bombs not half a mile from his house. He lived in a bungalow set back from the Garlochhead Road, near the Marina. It stood elevated from the road halfway up the hillside, a long, expansive building painted cream, with double glazing and solar panels, and a garage big enough to accommodate an articulated lorry. Charles Stuart's front door was kicked down at 5.30 a.m., Friday, 5th November.

Montgomerie had been on dawn raids before. He knew that arresting bleary-eyed suspects in their pyjamas was a lot easier and safer than making an arrest at 11 p.m. when the bars are shutting. But he also knew it was an operation not to be undertaken lightly, he knew that human nature is infinite in its variety, that it can spring surprises when least expected. Ray Sussock took charge of the operation. He had men in the garden, men behind the house, men in the lane at the side of the house. The cars and Transit van were parked at the bottom of the driveway. Sussock and Montgomerie stood at the front door. Behind them were three constables. After fifteen minutes there was still no response to the doorbell. The door was a light timber-framed apparatus with a glass panel. Montgomerie smashed the glass with a truncheon and took off the lock, but couldn't reach the bolts at the top and bottom of the door. He put his foot to the frame and the door splintered inwards.

Strathclyde Police

Witness Statement

Witness: Sylvia McElroy.

Address: c/o Jones Guest House Gll

Date: 4.11   *Case Officer*: DC Montgomerie

Div: P

I work as a waitress in the Bells of Hell Club in the Broomielaw. At approx. midday on 4.11 in the company of DC Montgomerie I witnessed a man whom I know to be Mr Charles Stuart hand a small parcel to another man whom I now know to be Mr Gavin Floyd. Mr Floyd is a frequent luncheon guest of Mr Stuart's and I have witnessed Mr Stuart handing a parcel to Mr Floyd on earlier occasions.

Sylvia McElroy

STRATHCLYDE POLICE

WITNESS STATEMENT

Witness: Charles Stuart

Address: 'Benbecula' Helensburgh

Date: 5.11   *Case Officer*:   DC Montgomerie

Div: P

I am Charles Stuart aged 53 of 'Benbecula', Helensburgh. I am managing director and majority shareholder in the civil engineering company of Torvaney-Stuart.

I have known Gavin Floyd for approximately two years in which time he has sought my advice on financial matters. I am aware that he is the Chairman of the Roads and Public Highways sub-committee of the Regional Council General Works Committee, which has approved a number of Torvaney-Stuart tenders. I have not offered Mr Floyd any financial inducement to favour Torvaney-Stuart tenders.

On November 4th this year I had luncheon with Mr Floyd at my club, the Bells of Hell in the Broomielaw. I handed Mr Floyd a sum of money totalling £350 which

Mr Floyd had agreed to keep for me. The money belongs to Torvaney-Stuart and is slippage money from the company accounts which forms part of my personal income. In handing the money to Mr Floyd's safe-keeping I was hoping to reduce my personal taxation liability. Mr Floyd has obliged in this way before but has never known the reason for which he was asked to mind the money.

I have known Mr McFarlane for six months. He approached me in the Bells of Hell using a Dutch name which I don't recall. It was only recently that he told me his name was McFarlane. Since then he has been pressing me to either loan him money or let him invest in Torvaney-Stuart. I have never entered into any kind of contract with him.

Very early yesterday morning he telephoned me asking for help to raise capital for a venture, a parcel delivery service, I believe. I wasn't interested but did arrange for him to meet Mr Floyd who I knew had been looking for a business opportunity for some time. They met at the Bells of Hell at lunchtime yesterday. I do not know what agreement if any they entered into.

Charles Stuart

STRATHCLYDE POLICE

WITNESS STATEMENT

Witness: Gavin Floyd

Address: Glamis Causeway G34

Date: 4.11   *Case Officer*: DC Montgomerie

Div: P

I am Gavin Floyd and I am forty-nine years of age. I am employed as a clerk with North Western coach and Car Hire. I also serve on the Regional Council and am Chairman of the Roads and Highways Sub-Committee.

I have held this office for the last three years.

Shortly after I became the chairman of the committee Mr Stuart approached me and befriended me. He introduced me to the business community and gave me advice about how to start out myself. I attended parties at his house and also attended other social functions with him. At one party when I had had a lot to drink Mr Stuart took me to one side and asked me to do him a favour. He said that his company was having a difficult time and as I was now a friend of his I had to help him out by getting his firm's tender accepted by the council. He said that this was the way things were done in the business world. Then he gave me £100 and said there would be another £100 if the tender was accepted.

There were further payments for similar reasons over the next three years. I have received nearly two thousand pounds in that time from Mr Stuart all for the purpose of using my position to favour Torvaney-Stuart tenders.

Mr McFarlane was introduced to me by Mr Stuart. I met him for the first time today. Mr McFarlane had Mr Stuart's recommendation and was looking for a backer for a business involving rapid transport of parcels and documents. Mr McFarlane said he had one thousand pounds of his own and needed a further thousand that day. He informed me that an acquaintance of his had two 15-cwt vans which he was willing to sell, at a good discount, for two thousand pounds cash.

Mr McFarlane had to have the money that day, he said, because a rival buyer was coming over from Edinburgh the next day. I had been advised to bring some money and with the money that Mr Stuart had given me I was able to give Mr McFarlane one thousand pounds. I also gave him a further one hundred pounds so that he could register the company. I also gave him my address so that he could contact me when his solicitor had drawn up the contract.

Gavin Floyd

TELEX

ROYAL NETHERLANDS POLICE
AMSTERDAM
1134100

5.11 AT 06.00

INSPECTOR VAN DER VEEGHT
P DIVISION STRATHCLYDE POLICE

REF: DONALD MCFARLANE ALIAS JAN NIEUKIRK ALIAS SMILER,
THE

POSITIVE ID OF PHOTO OF SUBJECT AS PERPETRATOR OF MURDER
OF FRANS BAKHUIS. WITNESS WILLING TO TESTIFY IN COURT.
PLEASE APPREHEND WITHOUT DELAY. EXTRADITION
PROCEEDINGS WILL START IMMEDIATELY FOLLOWING ARREST.

Donoghue dropped the Telex on top of the witness
statements and looked across his desk-top at Van der
Veeght and Montgomerie, who both sat silently waiting
for his reaction. He tapped his pipe against his huge glass
ashtray. 'I think it's time we had our friend McFarlane in
for a chat' he said.

It was 10.20 a.m., Friday, November 5th.

CHAPTER 9

Murphy's Bar is a red-and-white quarter-gill bevvy bin
shoved halfway down a back street in Partick. Punters get
the big choice of wine or spirit and it's standing room
only. It's a bar where women and strangers are welcomed
with equal hostility and where 'Isiah' Mary stands by the
door with her head hung permanently on one side,
picking up three-quid tricks to take through the close into
the back court. At 11.10 a.m. on Friday, 5th November
there was only one punter in the bar. He stood at the

gantry and crushed the newly spread wood-shavings under his right boot-heel. It might have seemed the action of a man with not much on his mind before the whisky got to him. But the Smiler was a deeply worried man. He'd been a worried man before, but this time he was in fear for his life.

It had been in his letterbox that morning, inside a brown envelope that had been trapped by the letterbox flap. A .38 cartridge: the kiss of death from the Triad. He knew it allowed him six hours, maybe eight, to sort out his personal effects, maybe write a simple will, write a few letters.

He wasn't bothered any more about how they had found out, what mattered was that they did know what he'd done to the last shipment, how he'd set up Domino Pahl. He had tossed the bullet aside, pulled on an all-weather jacket and an old cloth cap and had left his flat in Hyndland Crescent. He had walked in the grey morning light to some derelict tenements and had sat in a damp close getting his head together.

He knew that Donald McFarlane was dead and that the Smiler was alive. They called him the Smiler because he never did, he was tight-lipped and cold-eyed. He was a loner because a partner was double the burden, double the trouble. The Smiler's world was gin joints, gutters, rough sleeping in empty houses, it was travel by night, keep your back to the wall and trust no one. At eleven he went to Murphy's and stood at the gantry where he could see the door in the mirror above the till and where he was near the kick-bar of the fire exit. There was a bulge in the inside pocket of his jacket caused by another brown manilla envelope, but this one held good news: the eleven hundred quid the sucker had given him.

Just like that.

He wanted a shooter, a blade at the very least. He knew he had to book out of this city, but he knew he had to do it right, like he'd learned, blending wherever he went, stealthily, silently, fleetingly, cat-like.

The minute hand of the old clock behind the gantry rested on the quarter-hour. He reckoned that from noon he was on borrowed time.

He waited until midday. It seemed like the starting-gate, and the dull chime the starting-pistol. He put his glass down on the bar and walked across the wood-shavings and out into the street. The sky was blue, the clouds were low and white, the wind was chilly. It sliced into his clothing and made his jacket collar flap against his cheek. It wasn't raining. He was thankful it wasn't raining, the rain never suited him. Apart from his personal taste were the practicalities: rain was uncomfortable and discomfort takes the edge off cunning; if he had to run it was better to run on dry concrete than on greasy urban pavements; he could see further when it wasn't raining; he could walk over open ground without leaving tracks. He had been hunted, he had been the hunter, now he was the hunted again and he was pleased it wasn't raining. That was one thing that he had going for him. The other was his health: he was in good shape, he had exercised regularly, never smoked, never drank to excess. His body was lithe and muscular, if he had to move he could move fast, if he had to fight he could fight hard. Then there was the cash, all he would need for this emergency; it meant he didn't have to knock an old lady over the head in order to eat. There was his track record; he'd been on the run from the police in three different countries, hiding in barns, submerging himself in mud, putting up in four-star hotels. He knew the key to successful evasion: move, move, move.

As he walked there developed a spring in his step There was a saying, 'You can never escape the Triad.' The Smiler reckoned it wasn't a hundred per cent true. He didn't know any saying that was a hundred per cent true and he didn't see why this one should be any different. There had been rumours of people slipping away in the night, but they were few and nobody had seemed to know them personally. Still, it had been done, and the Smiler was going to do it again. He was in his native city. He knew Big G as well as most Glaswegians and he certainly knew it better than anybody from the Dutch East Indies, or some Teutonic thug hired in a Rotterdam night-club.

He bought a meal at a burger bar. He ordered a double with chips and had it embellished lavishly with vegetables. His drink was a large coffee. He was off alcohol now, for the duration. He relaxed and didn't hurry the meal. When you move, you move steadily, you don't rush and draw attention to yourself. He didn't bother to look about him, searching for the assassin. He knew that they would make themselves known to him, he knew how the Triad worked. If he was killed it would not be by having his head blown off by a high-powered hunting-rifle fired from a great distance, it would be at close quarters, and probably after a period of incarceration. So the waiter was the waiter, the well-dressed woman was a well-dressed woman. If either had more sinister private lives it didn't concern him.

He began to wonder whether he should leave Glasgow at all. There was an advantage in staying in the city he knew best, but there was also an advantage in moving on, not to the big cities where he would be expected to go, but to some obscure little place, a one-horse town where he could live quietly and be able to rapidly spot the stranger. But suddenly the thought of spending the rest of his life in Alloa filled him with dread.

He left the burger bar and looked for a place to buy a gun. He knew that in Glasgow guns are not difficult to come by. He knew that if you walked anywhere near the underworld in any large city there was always someone who knew someone who could lay his hands on a shooter. Only in Glasgow it was easier. You just had to go to the bars where the sailors went, especially if there was a ship just in from the States.

He went to Buchanan Street and took the clockwork orange to Cessnock. It was a quiet period of the day and he was alone on the platform. That was an additional bonus, a confirmation that they did not yet know of his whereabouts. He wondered about them. How many of them were there out there? How would they approach him? Who would it be? Of one thing he was certain, it wouldn't be the one who had spent the last five nights in his flat discussing transit details, who would not give her name. He heard the sound of the train in the tunnel, saw the leading light illuminate the track. The train gave a whistle which seemed more like a strangled shriek, burst out of the tunnel and slowed to a stop at the far end of the platform. It was composed of just two coaches, brightly painted, and minute compared to the London or Paris subway trains.

The Smiler walked out of Cessnock tube station and turned left down the main drag. He walked towards the cranes. He was looking for a bar, not just any bar, but the right sort of bar. There were small shops and rusted tin posters, relics from the 1950s; children were playing, and the paving-stones rested at odd angles as though they had been disturbed by an earth tremor. He saw a bar which looked about right. It stood on a corner and had wooden panelling below a series of opaque windows. It was called The Shack.

The Smiler went in. It was a one-roomed bar entered by the steel door at the corner. It had a small gantry, most of the floor area being taken up by wooden tables and chairs which were fixed to the floor with chains. There were a few punters in the bar, mostly old guys with tams who sat silently studying the glasses in front of them.

The guy behind the bar was a bald-headed bruiser who looked as though he'd had a slice of every piece of action since the Spanish Civil War. The lines on his face looked as though they had been chiselled, his arms were as thick as telegraph poles, his shirt was open at the collar and revealed a forest of grey hair. The Smiler noticed the barman's eyes were small, very small for a skull that large.

'So what I get you?' said the man.

The Smiler said he'd take a lager and dropped a Cydesdale Bank quid on the gantry top.

'Know of any shipping movements?' he asked, taking his change.

'What shipping movements you want to know?'

'Looking for a Yankee.'

'For why?' The barman leant forward and rested his elbows on the bar.

'My business, Jim.'

'So now it is mine.'

The Smiler shook his head.

'So you won't tell me, I can't talk.'

'I can find out elsewhere.'

'OK, so find out elsewhere, but here's the right place for you. I know the look in your eyes, young one. I have seen it a thousand times. So what for you want a Yankee. You want to stow away? That isn't easy done these days.'

The Smiler shook his head.

'So therefore you must be looking for a pistol.'

The Smiler nodded, slightly.

'I thought it was that. I also think you want it to defend yourself.'

'Right again,' said the Smiler.

'OK. Yesterday night I had some guys in off a ship. They had come from Cuba and called at Baltimore and New York. It is an old rust-bucket with the Liberian flag. It is tied up in Princes Dock, centre basin. They hadn't eaten well on the trip and hadn't picked up good money.

They were selling things, ganja, machetes, some had jewellery.'

'What were they like?'

The man shrugged. 'Some were black, others white, others in-between.'

'Where are they now?'

'Sleeping it off, friend.' He turned and looked at the clock behind him. 'But now it's one-thirty, perhaps they're taking the hair of the dog. Go somewhere near Princes Dock, try a bar called the Square Rig, turn left from this door, walk three streets towards the city centre, turn again left. You will see the bar.'

The Smiler thanked the man and left the bar, leaving his lager untouched.

The Square Rig was a concrete bunker set on the corner of some waste ground next to the customs shed. Above the customs shed the Smiler could see rust and paint flaking off the white superstructure of an old-style cargo ship, the type with the funnel in the middle and rows of derricks fore and aft of the bridge. It was the only sort of vessel which came so far down the Clyde these days and there were not that many of them left. The ship was called the *São Paulo*.

Inside the bar the Smiler took a Coke and sat on a wooden bench, resting his glass on the wood and metal table in front of him. The table was too high and too narrow to be comfortable, but right then the Smiler wasn't greatly interested in comfort.

Right then he was greatly interested in a group of three men who sat gingerly sipping beer. The one who was facing the smiler was a handsome West Indian in his twenties and, thought the Smiler, very definitely the leader of the group, sitting forward and talking while the other two sat back and stayed dumb. The other two had their backs towards the Smiler. They were small and had lighter-coloured skin. The Smiler reckoned they were Puerto Ricans.

The gantry was run by a woman wearing a black dress and a string of imitation pearls round her wrinkled neck. The only other person in the bar was an old guy in a bonnet and scarf who was mumbling to himself. The Smiler turned again and looked at the three men, but not so as to faze the West Indian, who had become aware of his presence.

Presently the Smiler got up and walked across the floor and stood by the men's table. They stopped talking and looked up at him, their eyes narrowing. They were in a strange bar in a strange town but the rules were the same all over the world: if a guy wants in he's got to have something to sell, or money to spend.

'You want something, mister?' asked the West Indian slowly and quietly, so quietly that the Smiler scarcely heard him.

'You guys off that ship?'

'Who wants to know?' It was the West Indian again.

'They call me the Smiler.' The West Indian seemed to be doing all the talking, so the Smiler addressed him. 'I heard that some guys from that ship had things to sell. I'm looking to buy.'

'There was a big crowd around the bars last night. Maybe we don't have what you want to buy.'

'Maybe you don't. Maybe you know where I can get it.'

'Wutch yo want, man?'

'Things,' said the Smiler. 'Couple of things.'

'What we have is strictly for cash sales,' said one of the two smaller men, suddenly, unexpectedly, authoritatively. He had rapidly darting eyes and the Smiler quickly saw him and not the West Indian as the brains. There was also a look which flashed across the man's eyes which told the Smiler that as well as being the brains, the little guy was also the danger area.

'That's cool,' said the Smiler to the little guy.

'So what you want, white boy?'

'Like I said, couple of things.'

'Maybe you'd better slide in next to Toucan.'

'They call me Toucan,' said the West Indian.

The Smiler sat down next to Toucan, placed his hands on the table top and then clasped them together. 'I want a shooter,' he said. 'Plus ammunition.'

'What sort of heat you have in mind, white boy?' said the little guy. Sitting diagonally opposite him, the Smiler saw the leader of this pack to have a thin weasel-like face with some expensive gold crowns inside his mouth.

'What sort of heat you got?'

The Puerto Rican grinned widely but said nothing.

'OK,' said the Smiler. 'I need a hand-gun, with ammo.'

'You need, bro.' The Puerto Rican grinned. 'Y'all hear that, white boy he don't just want, he nee-eeds.' The other two men laughed and held out their palms for the Puerto Rican to slap.

'You have money, white boy?' The laughter suddenly stopped.

'Uh-huh.'

'How much money you got, white boy?'

The Smiler remained silent and stared impassively at the Puerto Rican. Their eyes met, the cold calculating stare, the mutal recognition of kindred spirits.

'OK,' said the Puerto Rican and turned to the man beside him. 'Nicosia, you go and fetch that piece stashed in your locker. Bring the man twenty rounds of .38.'

The third man slid off the bench and left the bar.

'So we have Toucan and Nicosia. What d'they call you, boss?'

'Never you mind what they call me, Smiler man,' said the Puerto Rican. 'Never you mind at all, bro. What you getting is top quality, and clean. Colt Navy revolver, .38, four-inch barrel. Good for close work.'

'Let's talk price.'

'No need, white boy, it's a fixed price, fifty British pounds for the piece, fifty for the ammunition.'

'That's heavy bread.'

'Take it or leave it.' The Puerto Rican shrugged his shoulders.

'OK,' said the Smiler.

'It's a solid little piece, man,' whispered the West Indian. 'Just waiting for a buyer.'

'He don't need no pat on the back, Toucan,' the Puerto Rican wailed. 'I don't sell no shit, Toucan man.'

'I know, Shelby, I know you don't sell no shit, the man here wants reassuring.'

'Hi, Shelby,' said the Smiler.

'Big mouth! Toucan man, you're a big mouth, reassure, shit. When you quit the sea you should be something nice like a Welfare Officer.'

'Stay cool, bro.' Toucan appealed to him.

The Smiler rose and left them at it. He went to the toilets, took out a hundred pounds from the brown manilla envelope and transferred it into the outside pocket of his jacket. He returned to the table.

'You boys like a drink?' asked the Smiler.

He bought them a lager each and stuck to coke. Nobody spoke and the Smiler was glad, he could use time out to get himself together. He had food in his belly, he had money, he was getting a shooter, next thing he needed was a doss, somewhere to operate from.

Nicosia burst into the bar and came over to resume his seat. He sat panting, catching his breath in gulps. The Smiler was amazed the man had run; running in the docklands is all you have to do to make the polis act on suspicion, m'lud. Nicosia could have brought the law straight to the Square Rig, and, next to the Triad, the law was the last thing the Smiler needed.

'You got it?' asked Shelby.

'Sure I got it,' panted Nicosia. 'You think I'm dumb or something?'

'No comment,' said the Smiler.

'You say something, white boy?' Shelby eyed him coldly.

'Oh no . . .' The Smiler shook his head. 'Where is it, this solid little piece just looking for a buyer?'

'Inside my jacket,' said Nicosia.

'So let me see.'

'You dumb, boy? This is serious jail-bait, white boy. Serious.'

The Smiler glanced round the bar. The old guy had fallen asleep and was shuddering as he snored, but the barmaid in the black dress was perched on a stool under the spirit rack and was eyeing the group, vulture-like.

'OK,' said the Smiler. 'Where?'

'There's an old warehouse near here.'

'There's a lot of old warehouses near here, this part of the city is dying.'

'It's not so dead as some places I've seen. OK, the one we mean is down the street away from the customs shed. We used it yesterday for a transaction. We'll go now.'

'No we won't.' The Smiler didn't move. 'There's three of you, one of me. You could jump me.'

'We could . . .'

'But you won't; save your breath, I've heard it before, Shelby man,' said the Smiler. 'Just two of us go. Me and Nicosia.'

'Na. You could jump him.'

'I could . . .'

'But you won't,' said Shelby. 'You don't trust so easy, white boy. You're a lonely man.'

'I'm a loner,' said the Smiler. 'There's a difference.'

'You stand to be a loner one piece down 'less we can arrange something.'

'You stand to be a boss man carrying a lump of jail-bait

when you could be carrying a hundred green ones.'

'OK, white Smiler man. You go with Nicosia and Toucan.'

The Smiler shook his head.

'So what's wrong with that, man?' the Puerto Rican shrieked. Smiler recognized the type, rodent-like, over-friendly, short fuse. 'That's a big, big concession.'

'It's no concession.' Smiler stayed calm. 'Toucan is a big guy and Nicosia has a shooter.'

'So what you want? You're getting to me, white boy. I begin to smell shit.'

'I'll go with you and Nicosia. Toucan keeps his flesh where it is. Otherwise it's no go. It's not that difficult to get shooters in this city and you're beginning to price yourself out of the market.'

'OK, white Smiler,' said Shelby coldly. 'But don't get too wise, bro.'

'So let's go.'

The Smiler followed Nicosia and Shelby out of the bar and into the street. They walked two hundred yards along a deserted street lined with dockyard buildings — tall, imposing, quiet — and entered an empty warehouse. It reminded the Smiler of Bauermeister's operation, except that this building really was falling down. The iron was rusty, the roof was hardly there, water dripped every-where and there were puddles big enough to please a flock of geese. It smelled musty, it echoed their slightest noise. The Smiler was the last of the three to step through the large doorway and as he did so he glanced back down the street and caught a glimpse of the huge Toucan leaping for cover behind a protruding wall.

The Smiler knew then for certain what he had suspected: he was being set up. He was taken for a sucker to be ripped off. Mugged.

He had to decide what to do and he couldn't defer the decision until the next day. If he bolted he'd get away, no bother. If he went in he stood to lose a lot more than the eleven hundred quid, but he stood to gain a shooter, if there was a shooter. He went in. Those West Indians can sprint, boy, he reckoned he had fifteen seconds at the outside before Toucan's fifteen stones joined the party. The Smiler kept his eyes on Nicosia. If there was a shooter Nicosia had it. Just inside the door the two Puerto Ricans turned and faced him, grinning.

'Where's the money, white boy?' asked Shelby.

'Where's the shooter?'

'Show the man the piece, Nicosia.'

Nicosia slid his hand inside his jacket and pulled out a revolver. The Smiler waited until he could see the butt and took one step forward and brought his boot up into Nicosia's balls. As Nicosia crumbled the Smiler brought his boot up again and caught the man square on the jaw. He didn't wait to see him go down. He turned to Shelby. Shelby was crouching, there was a glint in his eye and a knife in his hand. The Smiler didn't see where he had kept the knife but then that was the nature of men like Shelby, they can conjure knives out of thin air. Fast.

They circled each other. The Smiler could hear Toucan's feet slapping on the cobbles, approaching fast. He needed that knife and to get it he had to make Shelby lunge, like they had taught him in the paras before they found out about his heart. The Smiler stepped sideways and made to reach for the gun lying near Nicosia's bloody head. Shelby lunged, a curious, inexpert lunge, running forward with arm extended, a tough guy who needed mindless heavies to survive. The Smiler grabbed the man's wrist and bent it back over the forearm. Shelby screamed and the knife clattered to the floor. The Smiler brought his knee up into Shelby's balls and grabbed the man's hair and brought his knee up again, this time into Shelby's face, busting his nose. The Smiler was crouching on the floor with a gun in one hand, a knife in the other and with two moaning bodies curled up like huge foetuses one each side of him as Toucan's hugh frame filled the doorway.

'Keep coming,' said the Smiler.

'Hey, man,' Toucan whispered, and then backed into the street and ran. The Smiler went to the doorway and watched the lanky West Indian until he turned out of sight towards the ship. He went back to where Nicosia lay and foraged in the man's clothes for the box of ammunition. He put the gun in the other inside pocket of his jacket, opposite the envelope containing the money, and slipped the ammunition into his jeans pocket. He didn't know whether Toucan had bolted to save himself or to bring up support. The Smiler didn't stay to find out. It was 2.30 p.m.

Ray Sussock brought two mugs of coffee into the bedroom. He laid one mug beside the bed and looked down at the finely formed girl laying there, with the duvet pulled just above her breasts. He enjoyed coming to Elka Willems's flat more than taking her to his own; not only was it neater, with greater luxury and warmth, but there was something about being in private property which made him feel more secure. It was a feeling he didn't get in his own flat, where everything from the lumpy mattress to the chipped crockery was owned by his Polish landlord, and he especially didn't get the feeling of security because fifty-four years of age is no time of life to be in a bedsitter. His own house in Rutherglen was mortgaged property which he had relinquished to one of the living dead.

He carried his own mug across the carpet and began to peel off his clothes, hanging them on the chair under the Van Gogh print. Elka Willems's flat was a room-and-kitchen in Langside; one room, one kitchen, a scullery, a toilet, but basically two rooms. A nice size for one person living alone, but originally designed for a family, with the

toilet shared with another flat. The cramped and
claustrophobic days of his Gorbals childhood were a bad
memory for Ray Sussock; he could still hear the screams
in the night.

He crossed back to the bed and slipped under the
duvet. She made room for him and slipped her arm
around his shoulders.

'Your legs are getting thin,' she said dispassionately.

'Thanks a bunch,' he grunted.

'No, I mean it, you looked like a potato on stilts when
you crossed the room just now.'

'So why don't you get yourself a film star? Why put up
with me.'

'Because film stars are boring egocentrics.'

'You have of course slept with a film star.'

'Of course. Actually he wasn't a star, but he was a big
name in the Stranraer Repertory Company and he
auditioned for a speaking part in a BBC Scotland drama.
He was lousy, in bed I mean, but he didn't know it, he
thought he was God's gift to women and there just weren't
ever enough mirrors in the room to keep him satisfied.
You're not at all like that, old Sussock,' she patted his
stomach. 'And you're quite good in bed.'

'That's me,' said Sussock sleepily. 'Still a sexual athlete
at fifty-four.'

'So what did bold Sergeant Sussock do this morning,
then?'

'Raided a guy's flat in Partick but he'd done a
moonlight. Left all his belongings, though. He hadn't
turned up for work either.'

'That was McFarlane's flat, I suppose?'

'Aye, connected with the Pahl killings. McFarlane's
wanted for murder in the Netherlands. Fabian's sworn a
warrant for his arrest but he reckons it might not be
enough to get him extradited because the chief
prosecution witness is a gaolbird in Holland.'

'That will please the dishy Dutchman.'

'Aye, he wasn't the happiest person I've ever seen when he found out that McFarlane had flown the coop. Him and Fabian are not seeing eye to eye at all.'

'So what now?'

'Well, we're putting a twenty-four-hour surveillance on McFarlane's woman friend and the forensic boys are going over her room at the Antonine this afternoon. Joe Soap here was left watching McFarlane's flat in case the bird comes home. I'm going back in at ten tonight and I'll likely be spending the night in Hyndland Crescent.'

'Tonight!' She held his arm. 'Ray, but you've just come off the early shift.'

'Lack of personnel. They can't spare a car either. So it'll be just me and a packet of fags, some chocolate and a radio, huddled in a close.'

'You did that all morning as well?'

'Aye.'

'I expect you're very tired.'

He said he wasn't that tired, not that tired at all.

CHAPTER 10

At 3 p.m. on Friday, 5th November the woman who had been seen in the company of Donald McFarlane left the Antonine Hotel and walked towards George Square. Detective-Constable Richard King was close behind.

The woman crossed George Square. She ignored the drunks and she scattered the pigeons. She walked into the foyer of Queen Street Station, bought a magazine from the newsagents, walked to the booking-hall and stood leafing through a brochure about the West Highland line. She carried herself well. Her hair was long and black, her legs seemed slender and were encased in expensive nylons. She wore a heavy fur coat and a matching hat which, together with her hair, obscured most of her features. In the booking-hall she half-turned towards King, who saw her to be of oriental extraction. But that, he felt, was no big surprise. The woman slipped the brochures into her handbag and returned to George Square, calling in at the Information Bureau to collect a Scottish National Orchestra prospectus.

The woman moved purposely but not hurriedly: there was a decisiveness about her but no sense of urgency. King had the impression of a very self-possessed personality. She left the Information Bureau and walked down Bath Street and into Buchanan Street. King followed her with difficulty; her slow walk in streets that were not as crowded as they might have been late on a Friday afternoon, and in daylight, made her a difficult subject for surveillance. She walked down the left-hand side of Buchanan Street Pedestrian Precinct, stopping at shop windows, occasionally glancing around her, but never giving the slightest indication she suspected she was being watched. She walked diagonally across the precinct and entered Fraser's department store. She spent an hour in the store, bought a handbag and a silk scarf, paying in cash both times. At 4.30 she left Fraser's and walked back to the Antonine Hotel, taking the long route along Argyle Street; presumably, thought King, because of the shop window displays.

In the hotel she took her key from the reception desk and walked towards the lift, turning to face the foyer just as the lift doors opened. She stepped in and the doors slid shut behind her. King phoned P Division from a pay-phone in the foyer. 'She's acting like a tourist,' he told Donoghue. 'She may be going to a concert, she may be touring the Western Isles, she's oriental in extraction. She spent a bit of money and did a lot of window-shopping.'

'She'll likely be going out this evening, so stick with

her,' said Donoghue. 'Do you have a radio? Good. Let us know when she's at least half an hour away from the hotel. I've got Forensic standing by, Jimmy Bothwell's been kicking his heels all afternoon; we're going to turn her room over. Properly this time.'

King replaced the receiver, crossed the foyer and sat in a comfortable armchair. He liked the hotel, it was a nice place to stay if you had the money, yet it also irked him, the self-satisfaction, the complacency. He picked up a copy of *Scottish Field* and began to read an article about salmon-fishing on the Dee, but he couldn't properly relax.

When the woman reappeared she was wearing a dark leather coat, a black corduroy cap and low-heeled, 'sensible' shoes. She dropped her key on the desk as she passed. King let her get through the swing doors and then crossed the foyer to phone Donoghue. 'She's on her way,' he, said, and hung up without waiting for a reply. It was 7.30.

The woman turned left on Ingram and right at the end of the street and walked down towards Glasgow Cross. She walked in the same manner as she had done that afternoon, purposefully but in no hurry. At the Cross she turned left into the Barrowland. King closed up, partly because he was afraid of losing her in the gloom, partly out of a sense of dutiful protection: none but the brave venture into the Barrows on a Friday night. She walked past the single-storey development; junk shops, second-hand clothing shops, wine and spirit bars, and headed out towards the demolition sites, where there were no lights, just a vast expanse of rubble and the occasional smouldering bonfire. King closed up further. Still the woman walked on, she didn't alter her pace, she didn't quicken her step out of bravado, or falter out of fear, it was the same slow dead march, one foot in front of the other, a deliberate, fearless, almost stalking pace.

A demolition site fire was crackling far away to King's right hand; mostly it was a solid glow of embers but occasionally a small flame danced in the dark and was gone again. He detected a faint smell of wood smoke. He reached into his pocket for his radio and halted in the bricked-up doorway of one of the few remaining buildings.

'King. Over,' he said as loudly as he dared.

'Receiving.' A female voice crackled on his radio.

'She's on foot in the Barrows, walking east,' he hissed. 'I reckon she's at least half an hour from the hotel now, even if she does manage to find a taxi.'

'Roger,' said the female voice.

King pocketed the radio and began to follow the woman. He quickened his pace, she seemed to have got a long way ahead of him in the short time he had taken to make the radio call and she was made more difficult to see by the wisps of smoke which hung across the road. He pressed on, the smoke was getting thicker but he finally glimpsed the woman, seeing the dull gleam of her coat a few hundred feet ahead. Then he saw a bank of grey cloud roll across the derelict ground where there was no fire and he realized with a jolt that it wasn't smoke. It was a fog.   •

Jimmy Bothwell crouched on the floor of the hotel room and scraped the seams of the shoes with a thin blade. The minute and sometimes not so minute particles of grit and dust fell into self-sealing cellophane sachets. He was red-haired and awkward in his movements, but he valued his job and performed his duties with diligence. Sometimes it was grisly, like lifting fingerprints from corpses, and it would involve working anti-social hours, but he'd never swap back to his old job as assistant in the chemistry lab of a secondary school. Bothwell replaced the last of the shoes more or less where he remembered finding it and began to sprinkle aluminium powder on the small bedside table. Also in the bedroom were Van der Veeght and Donoghue. Constable Hamilton stood outside the door and Montgomerie hovered in the foyer.

Van der Veeght opened the drawers in the dressing table, rifling the contents of each. Finding nothing to interest him he slid all three shut with one movement of his huge palm. Donoghue sifted through the coats and dresses which hung in the wardrobe.

'You think she is here to stay, Inspector?' asked Van der Veeght.

'She certainly brought enough junk to last her for a good long holiday,' replied Donoghue. 'Can't find anything out of the ordinary, though. You?'

'Nothing,' replied the Dutchman. 'Perhaps she is not coming back. Perhaps she's meeting McFarlane and they are going away together. Brazil perhaps, Great Britain does not have an extradition treaty with Brazil, I believe.'

Donoghue let the comment ride. 'Go over it again,' he said.

'I think something is not here?'

'What?'

'But perhaps in the bathroom.'

'What?' asked Donoghue again, irritated.

'Tampons.'

'What!'

'Tampons. For this amount of clothes you would think she would be staying in Scotland for some weeks. My wife will not go away overseas even for two weeks without tampons, even if . . .'

'I wouldn't worry about it,' said Donoghue with a finality that surprised Van der Veeght.

Van der Veeght would have argued it if Bothwell had not come out of the bathroom, wide-eyed and blinking. He was holding a leather wallet inside which was a hypodermic syringe and two black packages, one of which

had been torn open. A white powder spilled from it.
'What do you make of this, sir,' said Bothwell. 'It was in a
waterproof container in the toilet.'

'Treason and plot,' said Donoghue.

Donoghue poured the dregs of the coffee from the pot
into his cup. He apologized to the group for taking the
last of the coffee.

'It is difficult keeping awake after fourteen hours of
duty,' said Van der Veeght, sitting in the chair directly
in front of Donoghue's desk. He had undone his tie
and opened his shirt. 'For myself I have my second
wind.'

'Do you have your second wind, Montgomerie?'
Donoghue raised the cup to his lips.

'It'll come,' replied Montgomerie, standing reading the
report submitted by Bothwell and the Forensic Science
Laboratory. 'Reckon this clinches it,' he said.

'She's certainly got some explaining to do,' agreed
Donoghue, cradling his cup in his hands.

'She still in the Barrowland, aye?' Ray Sussock sat on a
hard chair next to Van der Veeght. He had just had six
hours' sleep yet somehow looked more tired than any
other person in the room. Donoghue hoped it was just
Sussock's deceptive appearance, the effect of the
fluorescent lighting on the lines on his brow, the loose
flesh under his chin, the silvery hair. It seemed that thirty
years at the coal-face, at the fag-end, was at last having
its effect on him.

'So far as we know,' said Donoghue. 'King hasn't called
in for a couple of hours. I've sent a patrol car to cruise
around there so he's got ready assistance if he needs
it.'

'He's probably lost her in the fog and is too
embarrassed to call in.' Montgomerie closed the reports
and held them at his side.

'I doubt it,' said Donoghue. 'Knowing King, I doubt it.'

'I hope we don't lose her too,' said Van der Veeght coldly.

'Too?' Donoghue put his cup down on his desk. 'What do you mean?'

'We have lost McFarlane, I have lost McFarlane. Now the woman is missing. I think you do not react enough to situations, Inspector.'

'I think you over-react,' Donoghue said slowly.

'I act.'

'So do I. I do not jump in with both feet.'

'McFarlane has been missing since late last night. What have you done?'

'We don't know that. We haven't seen him since late last night, he's not at work, it doesn't mean he's missing. He has no reason to suspect our interest, he didn't take any belongings with him. He will surface again and the woman will not be lost.'

'I do not share your confidence, Inspector.'

'Well, I'm afraid your lack of confidence will not alter my strategy.' He held out his hand. 'The reports, please.' He took the reports from Montgomerie and placed them on the desk top in front of him.

Van der Veeght thought it was a defensive move, a protective screen, just like the desk itself. It suddenly occurred to Van der Veeght that Donoghue wasn't as confident in command as he seemed.

'Tonight we move,' said Donoghue. 'We pick up the woman when she emerges from the Barrows. We'll have to wait till she gets back to the hotel because we'll never find her in this fog. Ray, you'll go back to McFarlane's close and let us know when McFarlane returns. It's a dry close, is it?'

'Aye,' said Sussock. 'It's a wee bit nippy, but it's dry enough.

'Good. You'd better get to it and relieve whoever's watching at the moment. Sorry we can't leave a car for you. Montgomerie, two warrants to apprehend, please.'

'Names, sir?'

'Use McFarlane and—what was the name on her passport?'

'Louisa Maartens,' said Van der Veeght.

'That's it, and have "believed to be an alias" typed after both names on the warrant. Inspector Van der Veeght, perhaps you'd like to get some rest, I think you'll get your much-craved action tonight.'

'I hope so, Inspector,' said Van der Veeght, standing. 'I do hope so.'

Alone in the room, Donoghue re-read the reports submitted by Bothwell and the Forensic Science Unit.

Strathclyde Police

> J Bothwell
> Forensic Assistant
> P Division

Inspector F Donoghue
P Division
Charing Cross
Glasgow   G3

Report on fingerprints lifted from Room 235 of the Antonine Hotel on 5.11.

One set of prints only in room. (Please see attached transparencies). Same print also found on hypodermic syringe. Hypodermic syringe, powder, samples collected from shoes, hairbursh, toiletries, etc. despatched to Forensic Lab 20.10 hrs 5.11.

> *J. Bothwell*
> *Forensic Assistant*

Strathclyde Police

> Dept of Forensic Science
> Glasgow   G3
> JK/CT
> 5.11

Inspector F. Donoghue
P Division
Charing Cross
Glasgow   G3

Report on samples brought by courier at 20.30 hrs 5.11 with request for priority processing and q.v. Pahl D P1132 Nov.

1. Sachets marked 'from shoes of suspect', contain particles of grit, dog hairs, and carpet fibre identical to those in Pahl household.

2. Hypodermic syringe. Plexiglass, Swiss manufacture. One ml Luer (219 x 1½). Contains trace of heroin in a very pure form.

3. Two sachets contain approx 200g (each) uncut heroin.

4. Samples taken from hairbrush and toiletries. Hair is female, natural dark, dyed blonde but at least nine months old. No trace of recently shed tissue could be traced in any of the artefacts marked 'toiletries'.

Of interest is the wallet which contains the hypodermic syringe and heroin. Cavities and indentations indicate that it contained a second syringe plus some (five?) thimble-sized phials.

I hope this information is of use. A more detailed report will follow. All artefacts to be returned by separate courier.

> J. Kay, BSc PhD
> 21.30 hrs 5.11

Donoghue closed the report and squeezed his eyes. He picked up the phone on his desk and asked that more coffee be brought to him.

It was 10.20 p.m.

At 10.15 p.m. Flora Campbell was edging her way through Kelvingrove Park. She groped along the pavement like a drunk, alarmed that after so much time and so much energy she should have progressed so little. She felt she should have reached Sauchiehall Street by now; she wondered if she had taken a turning which was leading her deeper into the park. She was momentarily reassured by a car which passed her. Its headlamps, barely penetrated the fog, and its rear lights were greedily consumed, leaving her once again in an unpenetrable dampness.

She listened as the sound of the car's engine died away, and then heard a sound which chills every woman walking alone at night — a solid male footfall, not too far behind, somewhere in the fog, not getting any closer, not fading away. Just keeping pace, tap, tap, tap. She quickened her pace slightly and the footsteps behind stuck with her. At 10.20 p.m. the steps quickened, an arm was put around her neck, another hand clawed at her breasts. At five seconds after 10.20 she was sitting on top of her attacker, pushing an arm up the back, holding the hair and yelling for assistance. Flora Campbell was an off-duty police sergeant.

Flora Campbell's attacker was Madeleine Kelly. She was a large girl, big-boned rather than fat. She gave her age as nineteen and had residual traces of acne on her cheeks.

At 10.56 she was sitting in the interview room at P Division. Outside she could hear the angry horns of cars floundering in the fog at Charing Cross and a distant shudder of a diesel engine putting itself at the Cowlairs gradient.

'Let's have it,' said Elka Willems.

'What?' said Madeleine Kelly.

'All of it.'

'Why?'

'Don't push your luck.' Elka Willems tapped the pencil against the top of the desk. 'Madeleine Kelly your real name, is it?'

'Aye.'

'And you've never been in trouble with the police before?'

'No. How do you know?'

'I checked. I ran your name through the computer. We don't know of any Madeleine Kelly of 2365 Dalkeith Road, G 10. That's your real address, is it?'

'Aye.'

'What is it, lodgings?'

'It goes with my work. Hostel, sort of.'

'Where's your work, Madeleine?'

'This hotel.' The girl looked around the room; tiles, curled-up linoleum, high window, the bulb with no shade.

'Which hotel?'

'The Antonine, Ingram Street.'

'Oh yeah.'

'Aye.'

'So what do you do at the Antonine?'

'Chambermaid.'

'Making up beds, emptying out the rubbish bins?'

'Aye.'

'Aye,' sighed Elka Willems to herself, and began to fill in the statement form.

'So you like the ladies, aye?'

'Aye,' said the girl.

'Why?'

'Don't know.'

'Not too talkative, are you?'

'Don't know.'

'Tell me about the attacks, then?'

The girl shrugged her shoulders and looked blankly over Elka Willems's shoulders.

'With us, are you, Madeleine? I mean, you are in this world, aren't you?'

'Aye.'

'You're not in hyperspace then, tripping on the astral plane?'

'The what?'

'Kelvingrove Park. Does that place have any meaning for you?'

'I've been there,' said the girl with a smile.

'Roll up your sleeves.'

'How?'

'Roll them up!'

'I don't . . .'

Elka Willems reached across the table, grabbed the girl's right hand and pushed the sleeves of her combat jacket and her pullover above her elbow. She turned the arm over, looking at the back and the front. The arm was pale white, fleshy, with poor muscle tone. It wasn't scarred with marks left by dirty hypodermic syringes. Her veins did not stand out. The left arm was the same. There was no sign of the girl shooting up under her fingernails. Elka Willems leant forward and inspected the girl's eyes. The pupils were not dilated, the eyes were not bloodshot. The pulse was normal, a healthy seventy to the minute. Probably too healthy; a bit of anxiety from the girl would have reassured Elka Willems.

'You're not on any drugs, are you?' Elka Willems said as she resumed her seat.

'No,' replied the girl. 'Why?'

'It crossed my mind,' said Elka Willems drily.

'Uh,' said the girl and started to gaze at the light-bulb.

'You always this great patter-merchant?'

'Uh.'

'All right!' Elka Willems slapped her palm on the table. 'Wake up! Look at me! You've assaulted three women in four days, and you're in trouble. You could go to prison. Has that occurred to you? Have you heard of Forth Vale? It's on the other side of Stirling in the middle of a field in the middle of nowhere. You're spending the night in a cell downstairs and then tomorrow you are going there on remand. But you're not leaving here until I get a statement and I don't mean in monosyllables.'

'Mono what?'

'Jesus, Mary and Joseph!' Elka Willems stood, knocking her chair backwards as she did so. She left the interview room and slammed the door shut behind her. She locked it and stormed away down the corridor. Inside the room Madeleine Kelly continued to blink at the walls. It was 11.15.

Elka Willems returned an hour later. Calmer, caffeinated.

'I thought you'd forgotten me,' said Madeleine Kelly limply.

'That'd be a fine thing.' Elka Willems stooped to pick up her chair. 'Didn't like it here on your own, did you?'

'Didn't mind it. Didn't want to be forgotten.'

'Frightened of being forgotten?'

The girl nodded.

'There's a chance I might forget you, Madeleine,' Elka Willems said firmly.

The girl's jaw dropped.

'If you're not interesting to talk to I'll go away and forget you. If you want me to remember you, you'll have to tell me interesting things about yourself.'

'If I tell you about myself will you be my friend?'

'No,' said Elka Willems. 'But I won't forget you if you talk to me.'

'I don't like being forgotten.'

'Why?'

'Because of my mother.'

'Oh.'

'My mother used to forget me.' The girl was dead-pan, emotionless, not a hint of a chip, not a suggestion of bitterness, not a trace of a tear, not a glimmer of love. Flat.

'How did she used to forget you?'

'I don't know.'

'No, I mean in what way?' Elka Willems still had difficulty in remembering that Glaswegians will often use 'how?' in place of 'why?'.

'She used to put me in a cupboard. It was dark. She used to forget me.'

'You don't like being by yourself?'

'I don't mind. So long as I'm not forgotten. I can sit and wait if I'm not forgotten. I didn't mind being in the cupboard if she was screaming at me or kicking the door, then I could wait. It was when I was in the cupboard and everything was quiet outside that I didn't like. I didn't want to be forgotten.'

Elka Willems nodded, slowly.

'When did you leave home, Madeleine?'

'I got left behind when she flitted one night. I thought I'd been forgotten again but the day after the man from the catalogue came and asked me about money so I think my mother left me behind for to talk to him. Then I got took to a home and my mother never came back so I think she forgot all about me.'

'What then?'

'Left when I was sixteen. The Welfare found me a job in the hotel. They said it would help me, living in.'

'So you've been there how long?'

'Three years. I moved to the hostel last year. Before that I lived at the top of the hotel.'

'When did you start fancying women?'

'Dunno. Always did, really. One of the house-mothers was first. She cracked me across the face for it.'

'So you started to attack them?'

'Not at first.'

'When did it start?'

'A bit ago.'

'I'm likely to forget you if you're not going to be specific, Madeleine.'

'Specific.'

'Accurate. Exact. When exactly was the first one?'

'One?'

'Attack.'

'Just this last pay-day.'

'Thursday last week, was it? Are you paid on a Thursday?'

'Aye.'

'So Thursday last week?'

'Aye.'

Elka Willems wrote something in the file in front of her.

'That my file?'

'Indeed it is.'

'What did you just write?'

'Just that your first attack was never reported. Helps our statistical return.'

'What are you going to do with it, my file?'

'Well, we're going to put your statement inside it. What happens then is up to you. Whether it stays as thin as this and after seven years we discount these offences, or whether it gets thicker, depends on what you do.'

'Oh,' said Madeleine.

'So it was just the four, was it, the first lady last Thursday, the lady on Tuesday, the lady on Wednesday and the lady tonight?'

'Aye.'

'What did you want from them?'

'I just wanted to hold them.'

'Hold them?'

'You know, them.'

'You mean you wanted to fondle their breasts.'

'I suppose.'

'It seems to me that that is what lay behind these attacks.' Elka Willems sat back in her chair. 'I think you know what sort of relationship you want, don't you?'

'Aye.'

'Why did you dress as a man? Did you think it would attract the girls, or was it a disguise? It was a pretty stupid disguise; didn't it occur to you that we'd be looking for a man, initially, anyway?'

'I didn't really think. I got the idea from the man.'

'Which man?'

'The man at work.'

'One of the porters dresses in skirts, does he?'

'No.'

'What does he do then?'

'He dresses in skirts.'

'Madeleine, I just said . . .'

'No, he's one of the guests. He's been there all week. The Chinaman. He gave me twenty pounds not to clean his room. I do his room and all the others on that corridor. I never knew he was a man, right from the start I thought he was a woman, but I went in one day, I forgot, and saw him, he was undressed in the bathroom drying his hair with a towel. He didn't see me and I went out again, his room was a real mess. Anyway, it gave me an idea . . .'

Her voice faltered and fell silent as Elka Willems fled from the room. She listened to the policewoman's footsteps echo in the corridor and then sat silently in the room, blinking at the wall, listening for the sounds outside, hoping she wasn't forgotten.

*

Richard King was lost. He knew he was in the Barrows or maybe further out towards Bellgrove or Camlachie; maybe he'd wandered into Bridgeton. He tried to work out where he was in relation to the Gallowgate but the fog was so thick he had difficulty working out the position of his hand in relation to his head. He gazed up at the deserted shops which loomed out of the gloom, he passed an old lamp-post disconnected from the mains and came across a skip overflowing with refuse. He bumped into another human being.

'Where am I?' asked King.

'Don't know,' said the dark shape. 'Where am I?'

And again he was alone.

But he had not lost his quarry. When he couldn't see her he hurried recklessly through the fog until he fell within earshot of her footfall, tap, tap, tap. He couldn't work out this woman, this rich piece who put up at the smart hotels and walked in the fog round the depressed part of the city. Smart women don't walk in derelict parts of the city in the fog on a Friday night, they just don't. He reckoned she was a screwball, this one, walking purposefully, leading him round and round the Calton and the Barrows and not getting anywhere in particular.

The clicking heels led him past an open space, a demolition site; and the flame of a small fire to his right penetrated the fog. He followed the sound into an area where the buildings still stood but were boarded up and waiting for the big hammer. He couldn't see high enough to read the name of the street, which he knew must still be bolted to the buildings at the road juctions. He followed the heels past decaying closes and empty shops sheeted over with corrugated iron.

Very suddenly he could no longer hear the woman's heels.

Very suddenly it was very quiet and still. Even the lousy

fog seemed to hang in suspended animation. Still, quiet,
cold, lost. King stopped walking and listened hard, he
could hear nothing. He walked slowly forward, treading
softly, stopping frequently to listen. Not a sound, just
uneven pavements and gaping closes of derelict
tenements.

He tried not to panic . . . leading him, she was . . .

There was a noise behind him, he turned, a shape,
roughly human, a hand coming down, his hand went up,
an involuntary reflex action, a dull pain at the side of his
head, he began to feel himself falling a long way, swirling
with the fog as he went down.

CHAPTER 11

The Smiler ran from the old warehouse to the end of the
street. He then walked to Paisley Road West, looking
casual, with his collar turned up and his hands in his
pockets, keeping his head tilted slightly forward. Just a
city kid with a place to go and not out to cause anybody
bother. It was a passport which would buy him passage
down most streets in most cities. He hopped a bus to the
city centre and went in a coffee-bar near Central Station.
The aggro had left him shaken and he took coffee until
he'd calmed.

He left the café and went to the subway. He rode twice
round the circuit. It was a light time on the tube, only a
few people riding, and those in his coach changed twice
over. So far so good.

He wanted to survive and he had decided he wasn't
going to run. He'd learned the value of standing his
ground in his earliest days in the high-rise. The fifteen-
year-old hard men had given him a tough time and the
first thing he'd learned was, run or stay, you got battered

just the same. The second thing he'd learned was that
hard men's heads could be kicked in just like anybody
else's. After that it was OK.

The train ran into St Enoch's. Some people got off, a
couple of people got on. He reckoned the Triad was no
great shakes, nothing to build up a myth about. If he
could hit first he had a chance. Hit first, hit hard, hit
fast, just like he learned to do. He left the train at
Hillhead and crossed to the opposite platform and took
the tube back to Cowcaddens. He was one of only two
people who left the train. The other was a young Indian
in a turban who sprinted up the escalator ahead of him.
The Smiler glanced around him; nobody on either
platform, just an empty Tube station, posters in perspex
frames, and orange tiles, and the sound of the train
fading in the distance.

He left the station and walked under the fly-over
towards the centre of the city. It hit him like a dull thud
in the middle of his forehead, the first enemy, the most
dangerous enemy, the one he couldn't hit first, hard and
fast.

Fatigue.

The action and the drink before midday had caught up
on him. He forced himself to notice things, but he
couldn't prevent his eyelids getting heavy and his feet
dragging. He recognized the danger and knew he had to
rest. He dropped down into Sauchiehall Street and felt
safer among the crowds now that he knew he was not yet
being followed. He stopped at a phone-box and looked up
the cheap hotels and guest-houses in the Yellow Pages. He
made a list, scribbling with a ballpoint on a piece of
paper. Then he tore it up. Suddenly he felt he would be
safer up-market, in a hotel with stars on the outside and
chambermaids on the inside.

He went to the Buchanan on George Square. The clerk
at the reception eyed him curiously, not wholly

disapproving, not wholly suspicious, but edging in that direction. It wasn't difficult for the Smiler to see why the clerk wasn't overflowing with hospitality. It's not every day that guys in jeans and all-weather jackets and with mud on their boots book into four-star hotels.

'How long will you be staying, sir?' The clerk slid a booking card across the desk towards the Smiler.

'Just the one night.' The Smiler spoke softly, in a confident English accent.

'Any luggage, sir?'

'It's at the Central Station left-luggage office,' he said. 'I'll collect it later.' He filled out the form, giving an address in Hampshire and his name as Donald McFarlane.'

'Travelling in Scotland, Mr McFarlane?' The clerk held up the card, making no secret of the fact that he was reading the details.

'Going north,' he said.

'To the rigs?'

The Smiler nodded.

The clerk was pleased. He thought he should have seen it before. He knew that there comes a stage when a man is so wealthy he can dress down instead of dressing up, and there was only one sort of man who would walk into a four-star hotel looking as though he was dressed for a solid day's graft on a building-site and ask for a room. The clerk was called Everard Allcock and he wanted to quit the hotel business and make money on the rigs. He knew he hadn't the physique to be a diver but reckoned he could make his pile in the kitchens, dishing up the grub. Allcock pushed a key across the desk. 'Room 124, Mr McFarlane; enjoy your stay.'

A boy in a black jacket with a red collar showed the Smiler to room 124 and the Smiler gave him a five-pound tip just for the hell of it.

He shut the door before the boy could gasp his thanks,

and peeled off his jacket. He crossed the window and looked out on to George Square, the statues, the yellow and green buses, the dossers huddled on the bench passing the bottle. He stepped sideways to the wash-basin, stripped to the waist and turned on the hot tap. The scent of peat rose with the steam, and he inhaled deeply through his nostrils. That was the one thing that to the Smiler was Glasgow, and it was the thing he first noticed whenever he returned to the city. Home was smelling peat in the steam.

When he awoke it was dark and he reckoned he had been asleep for five hours, maybe six. He checked his watch: 00.45. He'd been out for ten hours. Jesus.

He sat up quickly. The sound of Friday-night, Saturday-morning Glasgow came into the room through the half-open window, the shouts and laughter, the traffic, the breaking of glass and the two-tones. He crossed the room to the door and listened. Hearing nothing from the corridor he opened the door. The corridor was long and empty. There were a few dim wall-lights which produced enough shadows to hide a company of Ghurkas, and the deep carpet and fabric wallpaper would muffle any sound quieter than an exploding grenade. The Smiler shut the door. The hotel was an alien environment and it worked against him. He'd rested; now it was time to book out. He washed again and dressed. His shirt felt tacky, but that was tough. Right then a clean shirt couldn't even dream of a priority placing.

He sat on the bed and checked the gun. It was a short-barrelled revolver chambered to take six cartridges. It was dry and needed oil, the mechanism was heavy to work, but it would do in the short term. He looked down the barrel, using the street lamp outside for light. It was dusty but not dirty. He could use the gun without fear of blowing his hand off. The ammunition he had taken

from Nicosia's pocket was the correct size. He put five
cartridges in the gun, resting the hammer on the empty
chamber, and put the gun back into his jacket pocket. He
was pleased it was a revolver. He preferred revolvers to
automatics. Automatics jammed and one dud bullet
could screw up the whole works, which was bad news if
you were in a tight spot. Automatics carried a punch, all
right, but you didn't need power for close work. He
pulled on his jacket and checked that the money was still
in the other pocket. Then he went down into the street.

He felt safer in the street, he knew the street and it was
wrapped in a dark November night. He walked from
George Square along George Street, occasionally glancing
behind him. He couldn't see anyone who was paying any
attention to him. He turned left at the end of George
Street because he knew there was only one place in this
city where he could crash.

Beyond Townhead lay an area of Glasgow which the
Smiler had always reckoned to have been bleak from its
inception. Fifty years on, Royston was a dismal area of
blackened tenements, cratered roads, dark empty streets.
A ghost town. Up a side-street which rose steeply from the
main drag and round a corner, sunk into the highest part
of the hill were the flats: rising twenty-five floors from the
gutter and garbage, three giant monoliths standing like
tombstones in crap. It was here that he had come after his
father's collapse, stepping out of a taxi followed by a
whimpering mother and twittering sister. The next day
he saw two dogs fight to the death. The spectacle was
watched by people who lined the pavement or leaned on
veranda railings. He was now part of them the big
Glasgow schemes, with their curious mixture of violence
and apathy.

The Smiler looked up at the flats. Only a few lights
shone through the fog. The flat were thrown up fifteen
years ago and had emptied rapidly, with folk voting with

their feet and others point-blank refusing to move in. Now only a few hardy, lonely or mentally subnormal people lived there, fighting a losing battle with the gangs and the glue-sniffers. Over to his left a bottle smashed, on his right something disturbed a heap of garbage in a close. Ahead of him a figure shuffled through the shadows.

He walked diagonally across the road and, under the shadow of the first block of flats, stepped on to the flagstones that lay in front of the entrance to the second block. The entrance was dimly lit by a long fluorescent lamp which was protected by a metal grill. The air was musty and the walls had been sprayed with graffiti: '1690', 'Fuck the Pope', 'Fenian Drummie'; empty crisp packets containing hardened solvent littered the floor. The Smiler avoided the lifts and took the stairs.

They were narrow and zig-zagged round the lift shaft to the top of the building. They were lined with unfaced breeze-blocks, which had also been liberally sprayed with graffiti. The Smiler read them until they became repetitive: it seemed that the spray-can gang were hung up on sectarian/sexual obsessions. The stairway stank of piss.

Above him, maybe up on the fifteenth or sixteenth landing, there was a fight in progress, or maybe some poor sucker was having his door kicked in prior to having his head kicked in. Or maybe they'd just inhaled a load of glue and were having a real good time. From the sound of it there were half a dozen guys and perhaps three girls. The guys were shouting, the girls were screaming and a door was banging and splintering.

The Smiler left the stairs at the tenth landing. It was a common gallery which formed a square round the column containing the lift and the stairs. Eight flats opened on to the landing. The Smiler groped through the gloom, turning to his left until he came to the door of

10/3. The door was ajar, but that was no big surprise; so were three other doors on the landing, the metal sheet that had been put over them having been torn down. They now lay on the landing. Three of the other flats had grey metal plates still in place over the doors and the eighth flat on the gallery actually looked to be lived in. He had the choice of four empty flats on this gallery alone, but he went to 10/3. It seemed logical.

He pushed the door open. It creaked on its hinges. He looked along the hall to the far room, into which the moon shone. The flat was empty, stripped of all furniture and fittings. It seemed appropriate to the Smiler that it should be empty, it had always been an empty flat, empty in its own way; no substance, no family life. His mother had been a woman under siege, lending her Benefit to pressing neighbours and never having the courage to ask for it back. She finally took refuge in Valium 10 and Carlsberg Specials. What exactly happened after she had started hitting the Carlsbergs the Smiler did not know. Early one summer's morning he had packed a few belongings into a sleeping-roll and left the flat, pulling the door quietly shut behind him.

He stepped over the threshold and inched his way down the hall towards the end room. He stopped and glanced at each room as he came to it; his sister's room, her room, his room, kitchen, bathroom. He reached the end room. It had been their living-room, decorated with odd sticks of furniture from the Salvation Army. From the living-room window you could look down on to the tightly packed tenements; in the middle distance was Sighthill Cemetery and on the horizon were the Campsies. He crossed the room and looked out of the window. Below was the fog, above were the clouds and moon.

Suddenly it occurred to him that the windows were intact. If the door was open the windows should have been put through from the inside long ago . . . A chill shot through his body, pulling the skin taut over his skull.

'Don't move,' said a voice from behind, calm, confident. 'My gun is pointed at your head.'

The Smiler remained still.

'Turn around,' said the voice. The Smiler recognized the voice but couldn't identify it. 'Slowly. Remember I can see you better than you can see me. Stay in the moonlight and close to the window.'

The Smiler turned slowly, keeping his hands by his side. At first he could see nothing but shadows, then his eye was caught by a faint gleam of moonlight reflected off a man's cheek. He half-closed his eyes and was finally able to make out a man, an Oriental man, sitting in the corner with his legs crossed, holding a gun which was pointing straight at the Smiler's head. The man had on a cowboy outfit; jeans, western boots, jacket, stetson hat. The effect was spoiled by his spectacles which, when he moved his head in a certain way, glistened more than his cheeks or the barrel of the gun.

'I have been waiting for you,' said the voice behind the gleam in the corner.

'That right?' snarled the Smiler. He was directly in front of the door, which opened inwards, towards the man. It was dark, all right, but the Smiler reckoned he had ten feet of dead ground to cross before he was in cover.

Dead ground.

'I have been waiting for perhaps one hour.'

'Tough.' Then he would need another three or four seconds to get the gun from his pocket. Even if the Sundance Kid didn't drop him before he'd moved six inches, the action that followed would be pretty quick stuff and three seconds would flash by like a millisecond. No. Stay cool.

'I'm used to waiting, it's not so tough.'

'So how did you know I would come here?' He didn't

look at the door. He didn't want to telegraph any plans.

'The hunted animal always returns to his lair.'

'I was planning on doing the hunting.'

'It hasn't worked out like that.'

'How did you know where to find my lair?' He leaned forward a fraction of an inch and flexed the muscles in his calves.

'Your sister told us.'

Sister. Us. The Smiler fell back against the wall.

'My sister.'

'Geraldine McArthur. She did not change her surname. Unlike you, she had no need of an alias.' The voice was emotionless, matter-of-fact. Cold. 'She is a courier. So we know your old home, so I knew where to come.'

'And who are you?' The Smiler's voice cracked. He was confused, frightened by his emotions; emotions he thought he had killed long ago. He hadn't seen his sister for fourteen years; why should he care about her, how did he know they really employed her? He saw the barrel of the gun drop slightly; ten feet, that's all, ten feet, the man was giving him a chance. No, he was doing more than that. He was letting him go. But he couldn't move. 'Who are you?' he said again.

'I am the lady you have been entertaining every night this last week.'

The Smiler was stunned.

'All those evenings in your flat, I thought you were an astute young man. I thought you might see through my disguise.'

'Jesus,' said the Smiler.

'The Glasgow police didn't, either. So you need not feel so ashamed. One of them followed me through the fog into a desolate part of the city. I hit him very hard with this gun. There is blood on the butt. I probably killed him.'

'So why me?'

'Why you, why your sister? Why throw it all away? You would have progressed fast enough without doing what you did.'

'What do you mean?' Stall him. Ten feet, that's all, ten feet, pull the gun and start shooting.

'You sabotaged the last shipment. You wanted Dominique Pahl's job, so what better way to get it than to—I think "set her up" is the phrase?'

'I was getting impatient.'

'You should have kept quiet about it.'

'I don't understand.'

'You told someone.'

'I didn't.'

'Last night one of our book-keepers in Rotterdam received a telephone call. It was anonymous. The word reached me just this morning as I was about to leave. Now I will have to get a later plane.'

'Jesus,' hissed the Smiler.

'Remember your sister before you run for the door. If you want to go I won't prevent you.'

'But my sister.' The Smiler sank back further against the wall. His sister. Silly, twittering Geraldine.

'Currently in Turkey.'

'You don't leave me much choice.'

'You have a choice. Not one I would care to make.'

The Smiler slid down the wall and sat on the dusty floorboards. 'OK.'

'Good. Now can you take off your jacket and roll up your shirt-sleeve.'

'So that's it.' The Smiler felt his stomach constrict. 'An eye for an eye. I'm going the same way as Domino Pahl.'

'No.' The man stood and crossed the floor and laid a canvas pouch down beside the Smiler. 'This will not kill you. It would be a shame to kill a mind such as yours. An express parcel service with legitimate backers. Excellent. I liked it very much. We shall probably use it elsewhere.'

The Smiler opened the pouch. It contained a gleaming silver syringe and three phials of white liquid.

'Please hurry,' said the man. 'We have a lot to do and I don't have much time. I have a torch, shall I hold a light for you?'

It was quiet up until 10 p.m. It usually was, even on a Friday Guy Fawkes night. After ten o'clock they started coming in thick and fast, in ambulances, private cars, police vehicles or on foot, staggering in with a handkerchief held over their wounds. The only compensation was that it got less hectic as the night dragged through to the dawn. At 10.15 the first casualties from the multiple collision on the Clydeside expressway began to arrive; the end product of fog, speed and alcohol. Two killed outright, three badly mangled. Then there had been a lull, it gave them time to attend to the odd broken arm, busted nose, cuts and bruising from battles in down-beat bars. Then there was the fire, oh, God, that was grisly. The walking wounded came first, they weren't so bad but the ones who had been trapped, Jesus, they just didn't look like human beings. And the smell from that one, a sick, sweet stench. At one o'clock they brought the young policeman in, a deep cut at the back of his head near his ear, he might be lucky but there might also be a lot of damage. For the moment he was sleeping in a side-ward with a constable sitting by the bed. At three there had been another car smash, not so serious as the first, two badly injured, but they weren't on the critical list. All in all it had been a bitch of a shift.

At 5.30 Fiona went to the ante-room where they had left the man. He had staggered in clutching his stomach and had been left with the two old winoes until he began retching, and had then been moved. She pushed open the grey plastic screens. The man was sitting on the floor gripping his stomach, groaning loudly, shivering yet pouring sweat down his temples. On impulse she knelt and took his arm and pushed up his shirt. Three deep holes in his flesh, more like craters than pinpricks, bloodless yet revealing layers of skin, formed a crude triangle at the top of his forearm. She pulled down his sleeve and patted his shoulder. She walked briskly to the reception desk and picked up the phone.

Montgomerie was covering in the duty-room. He had had a bitch of a shift too, but then that's nothing new for this city on a Friday night. Fights, knifings, the fire, the car-smashes, break-ins, drunk-in-charges, one murder (domestic). The big incident had been the attack on Dick King which threw the Division night shift into a state of solemnity. But feeling solemn didn't stop him feeling knackered. 6 a.m. was when the early shift started, and Montgomerie had let himself begin winding down at five. So when the phone rang at 5.45 a.m. he wasn't too amused.

He let it ring for a few seconds and then reached forward, grabbed the cord and pulled the receiver across the desk towards him.

'Happy Saturday, big Mal,' said the voice down the phone.

'Oh, God.' Montgomerie groaned and took his feet off the desk. 'This your idea of a joke, hen?'

'Don't call me "hen". You know I hate it.'

'Anyway, don't you have anything better to do? I'm furiously busy. This is the night shift I'm on, and I don't mean the night shift with the sun-worshippers.'

'Oh, very droll, very droll. And I don't believe you're busy. I'm not, so you can't be.'

'I don't see how that follows.'

'I'll tell you sometime. Anyway, how is it I can't phone you at work but you think you can phone me!'

'You have to choose the right time, but actually it's OK at the moment.'

'Is that because the smooth Edinbrovian bloody slavedriver is not around?'

'In a nutshell, yes,' said Montgomerie. 'At the moment he's upstairs slaving over a coffee-pot with the Flying Dutchman. Since they heard the news about Dick King they've been chasing their tails like mad dogs. Eventually they gave up and ordered some coffee.'

'Seems logical.'

'How is he?'

'Hairline fracture, no outward signs of brain damage but we'll do a complete scan tomorrow. He'll be off work for a bit. Have you anything out about his attacker?'

'We searched the area. It was difficult because of the fog, but we did come across a pile of woman's clothing in a stairway.'

'I don't . . .'

'Well, his attacker was a man in drag. We think he's now in trousers.'

'Well, anyway . . .'

'Ah,' said Montgomerie.'

'Are you all right, Malcolm?'

'Yes, why?'

'You said "ah", like you had hurt yourself.'

'I meant; never mind.'

'Well, there's this young man in one of the side rooms.'

'I didn't think you'd make a personal call at a quarter to six in the morning.'

'This young man,' she said, 'I thought you might be interested in.'

'Why?'

'Well, with reference to that book I decoded about heroin and that poor woman—God, what a situation to be in,—anyway, this young man has three marks in his arm, the sort made by syringes when they've gouged around searching for a vein. He's got stomach cramps, sweating, shivering, all the symptoms.'

'Of what?'

'Heroin withdrawal symptoms, Malcolm. He's doing what the heads call "cold turkey". I thought I had better inform the fuzz, man.'

'OK, OK. Look, hold on to him.'

'I don't think he'll be going anywhere,' she said calmly. 'All addicts are the same. When they haven't anything to shoot up they make a bee-line for the nearest hospital.'

'OK, OK. We'll be there in twenty minutes.'

Donoghue, Van der Veeght and Montgomerie were there in ten.

Fiona showed them to the side-room where the Smiler rocked on the floor, gripping his stomach. He was shaking and beads of sweat ran from his scalp.

'When did he come in, Doctor?' asked Donoghue.

'About three,' replied Fiona. 'We thought he was drunk so we left him in the waiting area to sleep it off.'

'Do you always let drunks doss here?' Donoghue looked surprised.

'It depends who's the Casualty Doctor, and on the weather and their clothing. When it's me and the weather's foul and they haven't a jacket or top-coat, like this young man, I let them stay. I argue it as preventive medicine. If I turfed them out they'd only come back with pneumonia and block a bed for two weeks.'

Donoghue grunted.

'But when he started shaking and retching we moved him in here on this,' she tapped the stretcher trolley. 'Later I found him on the floor and saw the pinpricks in his arm, well, hardly pinpricks . . . That's when I called Malcolm.'

'Oh, I see, you know DC Montgomerie?'

'Oh yes,' said Fiona, looking at Montgomerie and smiling.

Montgomerie cleared his throat.

'Well, after I saw the pinpricks in his arm I

remembered that book I decoded for Malcolm about that poor woman . . .'

'Sorry.' Donoghue held up his hand. 'You said you decoded it?'

'Yes. Then I gave it to Malcolm.'

Donoghue turned to Montgomerie, who was blushing deeply and looking at the rack of oxygen cylinders.

'I see,' said Donoghue drily. Then he knelt in front of the Smiler. The Smiler's eyes were glassy and filled with fear.

'McFarlane, is it?'

The Smiler nodded.

'But it was McArthur originally?'

Another nod.

'Call you Donny, can I?'

Again a fast, short nod. The Smiler's lips were closed but Donoghue knew the man was gritting his teeth.

'Some mess, eh, Donny?'

A quick nod.

'Bad, is it?'

Another nod.

Donoghue looked up at Fiona. 'Will it get worse, Doctor?'

'I don't think it's started yet,' she said, with a note of regret.

Montgomerie knew what she meant. Some years ago, when he wore long hair and Indian moccasins, he spent one summer on the road. He had arrived in Amsterdam. In the Youth Hotel two floors below Montgomerie's dormitory, a young American was doing cold turkey. He was making a sound that Montgomerie never wanted to hear again for the rest of his life.

'Can you do anything, Doctor?' asked Donoghue.

'We can use Methadone. But it is really only replacing one addiction with another.'

'What about a shot now?'

Fiona shook her head. 'I don't think he's bad enough. Really, I know he looks bad, but it will get even worse. I think Methadone is best used to take the edge off the withdrawal symptoms, otherwise he'll never recover.'

'You hear that, Donny?' asked Donoghue.

A quick nod.

'You want a smoke?'

The Smiler shook his head vigorously.

'Who did this to you, Donny?'

Another shake of the head.

'C'mon, Donny,' said Donoghue sharply. 'Do you know what they've done to you? 'Course you do. If you don't care about yourself, tell us who this bastard is so we can stop it happening to others.'

The Smiler shook his head. Fiona left the room.

The Smiler opened his mouth slightly. 'Can't,' he hissed.

'Can't what, Donny?' Donoghue put a hand on his shoulder. 'Can't what?'

'Can't tell,' he hissed again, and then gripped his stomach. His eyes screamed with pain.

'Can it get worse than this?' Donoghue turned to Van der Veeght.

'Yes,' said the Dutchman. 'So much worse.'

'Jesus,' said Montgomerie. He didn't know whether seeing was worse than hearing. He only hoped he wasn't around when the screaming started, it was bad enough being two floors above the agonizing howl, God knew what it was going to be like only two feet away.

'Why can't you, Donny?' Donoghue persisted.

The Smiler tried to speak. He shook his head instead.

'They've got the screw on you, Donny?'

A quick nod.

'Who?'

The Smiler stared at Donoghue. Donoghue knew the man wanted to scream, he knew that if he were alone with no one to hear he'd scream until he ruptured his vocal cords. Donoghue looked at the Smiler and, despite it all, recognized a brave man.

'Wife, girl-friend?'

A quick shake.

'Well, who then? Who's he got, Montgomerie?'

Montgomerie closed his eyes and tried to recall the Social Background Report in the file. 'Sister?' he said.

'That's it, Donny, they have your sister?'

A nod.

'Where?'

A glaring look which clearly said 'I don't know.'

'As a hostage?'

He shook his head again, vigorously.

'She works for them, maybe?' suggested Van der Veeght, leaning against the wall. Montgomerie felt the lack of emotion in the big Dutchman to be something more than professional detachment. But then maybe he'd seen it all before, maybe even ten times worse.

'That's it, Donny?' Donoghue said. 'They have your sister?'

A quick nod. Him or his sister. Donoghue felt he would have done the same.

'Where is she, do you know?'

A shake of the head.

'We've got the Pahl child,' said Donoghue. 'She's safe and well.'

'It is so, she is already with foster parents in Amsterdam. Also the other children.' Van der Veeght spoke loudly but the Smiler didn't hear him.

'We can grab your sister, Donny. Tell us where she is.'

'Don't . . . know,' he hissed, and gripped his stomach tighter.

'For Christ's sake,' said Donoghue to himself. Then, 'Did they nail you for your sabotage job, Donny?'

The Smiler nodded, quickly, violently.

'What were you, Donny? Some sort of hit-man?'
Donoghue pressed the man. 'It was you that killed the
one-armed man, wasn't it?'

The Smiler nodded again and between gritted teeth
said, 'Yes . . . yes.'

'Thank you,' grunted Van der Veeght.

'Don't mention it,' said Donoghue bitterly. 'Look at
him, will you? He's just as much a victim as anyone. He's
been in their clutches right along.'

'For us it has been the same,' said Van der Veeght. 'We
can never penetrate the organization. We can just fight it
where it appears on the streets, and it is always the same
people caught in the cross-fire, the users and the little
fish. We can never reach the organizers.'

'What does it take to make one human being do this to
another?' Donoghue stood up. 'They're animals.'

'Worse,' said the Dutchman.

'How in hell did they find out that he'd set up Domino
Pahl?' Donoghue appealed to the other two men.

'Loose mouth,' suggested Montgomerie.

Van der Veeght tugged an earlobe and said nothing.

'So who is coming to take his place?' asked Donoghue.
'First the Pahl woman, then him, now who? There'll be
one following him, surely.'

'Not necessarily,' Van der Veeght said. 'You may have
achieved something out of this. Glasgow has become hot
and expensive and there isn't a market here anyway. They
may use another port, Edinburgh, Hull, Newcastle.'

'I've never felt so helpless,' said Donoghue.

'You get used to it, Inspector.'

'Used to what?'

'What you are feeling, the anger, the frustration.'

The Smiler's scream made Donoghue's knees buckle.
All three men stepped back as the man began to writhe
and thresh on the floor. Montgomerie said, 'Oh no, not
again . . .' It was a scream which came from the depths of

the Smiler's stomach, and reverberated around the Casualty Department, bringing nurses running, wide-eyed, white-faced. Fiona pushed her way through the bodies, holding a syringe in one hand and a swab in the other.

'I prepared a small dosage in case,' she said, the calmest in the small room. 'If you'd just like to hold him, please . . .'

'Do you,' said Donoghue as he and Van der Veeght and Montgomerie stood, leaving Fiona to remove the needle and wipe the puncture with a swab, 'do you get used to this?'

'Probably we don't,' said Van der Veeght, shaking his head. 'Probably we are just so punch-drunk we don't feel anything any more.'

'What will you do for him?'

'For him?' Van der Veeght gave a slight shrug of his shoulders. 'Now that he has made a confession we can proceed with the extradition, and with the witness's statement his conviction for murder is—' he moved his hands in a circular motion—'I heard an expression . . . shut and . . .'

'Open and shut,' said Donoghue, nodding.

'So. In prison he will be treated and may recover if he had had only three shots over a short period. Also I think he will recover in prison because it will be a long time before he can get hold of any more heroin, perhaps ten or fifteen years. I think we have rescued something from this, Inspector.'

'We've rescued nothing! There's a murderer in this city and I want him.'

'There are probably a lot of murderers in this city,' said Van der Veeght. 'But I think this one has flown the coop. I think he only stayed to tie up this loose end.' He nodded at the Smiler, now sleeping and being lifted on to the stretcher trolley. 'Now I think he will be on his way back to the Netherlands.'

'Montgomerie, get on to the airport security, both Glasgow and Prestwick, have them check the passenger lists for all flights to Holland.'

'What name, sir?'

'Exactly,' said Van der Veeght. 'What name, what description? Why only check Glasgow's airports? Why does he have to leave today?'

'Jesus Christ!' said Donoghue.

The Aberdeen Mail growled up Cowlairs incline. The man sat in first-class, a slim travelling-case pushed into the recess behind his seat. His boots, which had been pinching his feet, lay on the floor, and his hat was pulled down over his eyes. The guard walked down the train and noticed the man. He recognized the type, an American oil-man, taxi from the station to the airport, big tips, loud voice. The guard eyed the man with distaste. He resented them coming over; it was Scotland's oil, not theirs. He stopped at the side of the man as the train cleared the tunnel and reached the flat.

'Ticket, please.' He shook the man by the shoulder. He didn't care that it was 6.30 in the morning and that the passenger looked tired. The guard could not see why he should be considerate to a man who was doing to Scotland what this man was doing. He shook the man again. 'Ticket, sir.'

The man stirred, jolted slightly, calmed, pushed his hat back and looked up.

The guard felt himself frozen to the spot. A chill swept up his spine and his knees weakened. He took his hand from the man's shoulder and forced himself to move, backing up the aisle. It wasn't the man's face which made him retreat—a hard face with a stiff mouth and a scar running down the left side—nor was it the man's hands, not resting but poised. It was the man's eyes. In the cold, penetrating stare the guard saw something he had never seen before, something he could not define but intuitively knew to be dangerous, poisonous, something horribly large and horribly evil.

Ray Sussock huddled in the close and shivered. He had eaten all his chocolate and had smoked his last cigarette. He sat there because no one had remembered to relieve him.